Gable

The Powers That Be

Book 1

Harper Bentley

Discover other titles by Harper Bentley:

CEP series:

Being Chased (CEP #1)

Unbreakable Hearts (CEP #2)

Under the Gun (CEP #3) coming March 2015!

Serenity Point series:

Bigger Than the Sky (Serenity Point Book 1)

Always and Forever (Serenity Point, Book 2) coming June

2015!

True Love series:

Discovering Us (True Love #1)

Finding Us (True Love #2)

Finally Us (True Love Book 3)

http://harperbentleywrites.com/

Dedication

To my grandmother
The strongest woman I've known

Acknowledgements

Many thanks to the book blogs who've reviewed my books and promoted them like crazy: Aesta's Book Blog, A Pair of Okies, Bedroom Bookworms, Cecily's Book Review, Mrs. Leif's Two Fangs About It Book Reviews, Sassy Southern Book Affair and Summer's Book Blog are just a few among gobs and I'm so grateful for the friendships that have grown from this! You guys rock!

To my girls who are always on standby and forever willing to read some of the silliness that I come up with. When I win the lottery, Lamborghinis for everyone! ;) You ladies never fail to amaze me with your patience and support. Thank you for everything!

To Anne Mercier who is the sweetest friend ever and is always there to let me bounce ideas off her even though she's busy writing kickass books. Thank you, dollface!

To Michelle Lee who gives me continuous support and always makes time to help me out even though she herself is busy writing away. Thank you, sweets!

To TC Matson who's friendship is one I truly cherish. And since your sense of humor is on par with mine, I look forward to many laughs to come. <3 you hard!

And finally to the readers because without you, I wouldn't smile nearly as much as I do. Thank you for that!

Summer, two weeks before class:

You know that feeling you get when you meet someone and feel as if you've known them for a lifetime? As if you're just connected in some way?

Yeah, that didn't happen the first time I met Gable Powers. Matter of fact, I didn't like him one bit.

Oh, I know about all the Powers boys now. I actually knew about them by the first day of school since it seemed as if every woman on campus couldn't stop talking about how each brother was just as gorgeous as the next, and things like, "Omigod! The Powers brothers are *so* hot!" or "Aren't they just *the* cutest you've ever seen?" were proclaimed almost everywhere I went the entire first week of school. From listening in on these chicks wax rhapsodic over these brothers, if they were anything less than Nick Bateman clones, well, then I'd be highly disappointed. But from their conversations, I learned the Powers were from Seattle, all of them went to Hallervan, Zeke was a senior who played on the football team, Lochlan was a freshman who was some kind of computer genius, Ryker was a sophomore wrestler and Gable was a junior. I had yet to figure out what his superpower was, but I can honestly say that when I first met him, I couldn't have cared less.

My up-close-and-personal with Gable Powers left me less than thrilled, and when I finally figured out who he was and said something later about it to my new roommate, I got a stare of disbelief which made me roll my eyes.

So here's how it all went down.

I'd answered an ad in the *Seattle Times* for a roommate. On my way to meet Amy (fellow sophomore who'd eventually become my new roomie), I'd had a flat tire and had to pull over in an area of the city I was unfamiliar with—hell I was unfamiliar with the entire friggin' place—and, of course, it'd been raining. As a farm girl, I knew how to change a tire, had no problem changing a tire, but per Dad's instructions, I called AAA and stayed in my car waiting for someone to show up, kind of feeling like a wuss for doing so. I knew I could've done it and been on my way in no time but I decided to let Dad parent me for a change. Not that he wasn't a good father; it's just that I was majorly independent.

Needless to say, I was a little surprised when a black pickup truck stopped behind me and a guy got out, almost immediately after I'd hung up with the auto service. I mean, I'd heard AAA was fast, but come on. The guy had come to the driver's side and when he'd tapped on the window of my little Honda, I'd seen the full sleeve tattoo on his muscular arm and my eyes had bugged out.

See, I'm from a small town in Idaho where everyone thinks tattoos are Satan's markings, which I know is ridiculous and is one of the many reasons I couldn't wait to leave that shitty little place, but I regret saying that when I'd seen his arm, I'd been a little on edge. The guy had stood there in the pouring rain while I contemplated what to do as I checked out the rest of him. He appeared to be over six feet tall and his entire body was ripped. Dang. I could see his abs all bumpy and defined through the wet white t-shirt that clung to him, and his rain-soaked jeans were stuck to what appeared to be muscular thighs. I'd then felt bad for ogling him as he stood there getting drenched, so I finally rolled my window down an inch and he'd bent to ask if I needed help.

And, my God, was he beautiful.

I stared at him as rain dripped from his straight nose to the ground. It drizzled down his high cheekbones where it met his strong, stubble-covered jaw, trickling to his chin before finally slipping off. The long curls of dark hair that framed his tanned face were dripping wet also, but it was his light brown eyes that held my attention, so expressive and soulful, lined in long, sooty lashes that were spiked from the rain. Damn. He was a total friggin' hunk.

"I've called Triple A, so no, thank you," I'd yelled over the rain through the cracked window.

He'd given me a sexy half grin, which made butterflies bounce off the walls of my stomach. "I could probably have it fixed before they even get their truck started."

I'd twisted my mouth to the side not really knowing what to do. I mean, if I agreed to let *him* fix it, *I* may as well just do it. "Uh, that's okay."

"Seriously. You wouldn't even have to get out, Rebecca. Just pop the trunk and I'll take care of it. You won't even have to lift one of your pretty, little fingers." The smug look he'd given me made me frown. A lot.

"Rebecca?" I asked wondering what he was talking about.

"Of Sunnybrook Farm. You know, all clean and wholesome. Prissy," he'd replied with a twinkle in his eye as he grinned fully now, his straight white teeth making him even more attractive.

What the hell? I'd grown up with two older brothers and I was anything but prissy. I could drive a tractor for chrissakes! "No, really, it's fine," I said through gritted teeth.

"Oh, c'mon. Can't have a helpless little lady like yourself out here all alone, you know. What are you, like fifteen?"

I blinked at how rude he was being which was when Kim Kardashian, Jr. had walked up holding an umbrella and wearing the shortest shorts I'd ever seen. The crop t-shirt she wore had so much cut off that I could see her braless boobs hanging out from under it and couldn't help but gape at how provocatively she was dressed. Then she'd whined, "What's going onnnnnn, Gable? God! These helpless little Daddy's Girls are so annoying! *I* could've changed the tire by nooooow! Leave the rich bitch alone and come onnnnnn!"

And that was the precise moment I think steam had shot out of my ears. I reached down and jerked up on the trunk release because *fuck that*. Then I'd thrown open my door and saw the guy jump out of the way. I walked to the back of the car, raised the trunk, pulled back the carpet and removed the jack then went to the side where the tire was flat, put the jack down and started loosening the lug nuts with the tire iron.

"Whoa! What do you think you're doing?" Jerkface asked, having come around to the side of the car where I was.

"Well, *Prissy Rich Bitch* here is changing her tire if you haven't figured it out," I muttered glaring up at him. And my eyes got great big when I saw that *both* his arms were covered in tattoos. Whoa. And why that made him even hotter, I had no idea.

That was when Kim, Jr. huffed and called the guy an asshole (with which I couldn't disagree), then she called me a stupid cunt (with which I totally took offense) and my mouth fell open as I watched her stomp back to the truck in her strappy wedge sandals, her ass cheeks totally hanging out from under her shorts. Wow. Classy babe.

"At least let me help you with that," Tattoo Guy said, ignoring his girlfriend.

The glare I'd given him had him holding up his hands to his sides in surrender, his eyebrows raised as he grinned at me. I know I must've looked like an idiot with my long, blond hair soaked and hanging in my face, my cute, white cotton romper, which was sticking to me everywhere and was now probably ruined as I'm sure were my very awesome, white ankle-high gladiator sandals, but I'd be damned if I was going to let him help me now after he'd made me out to be some helpless female.

When he hung around, I muttered, "Go away," as I positioned the jack and twisted the handle. Once I got the car jacked up, I realized he still hadn't left so I stood and turned to him, putting my hands on my hips. "What?"

The perusal he gave me made the butterflies kick up again. Stupid fucking half grin. I frowned at him then moved back to the tire and proceeded to take off the lug nuts. When I went to remove the tire itself, he stepped in, took it off the wheel and rolled it to the trunk as I followed, telling him I had things under control and that he should just leave now.

"Can't have you getting yourself all dirty, now can we?" He'd looked me up and down appreciatively and that's when I realized he could see everything through my outfit.

Shit! I hadn't bothered wearing a bra because the romper had a built-in shelf bra, and I'm sure I was giving him quite the show, knowing my nipples had gotten perky at his heated gaze. But now I had to own it. So taking a deep breath, I leaned into the trunk to remove the spare, but he pushed me aside gently and reached in for it. And, God, he smelled good, all fresh rain and hot man. Damn it.

"I can handle it. Really. Why don't you and Luscious take off?" I mumbled.

He set down the tire, appearing confused, then asked, "Luscious?"

"Your girlfriend. Isn't that her stripper name?" I smiled sweetly at him hoping that'd make him mad and he'd finally leave, but instead, he'd barked out a laugh then proceeded to roll the tire to the front. I sloshed through the rain behind him then watched as he finished changing it, none too happy about it.

"That's it," he said when he finished, putting everything back in its place in the trunk. Then his eyes landed on me, once again moving up and down my body making me want to cover myself with my arms but refusing to do so, and after wiping his hand on a rag held it up for me to give him a high five. "Nice working with you."

A high five? Really? Maybe he did think I was fifteen. "Uh, yeah," I replied moving my hand slowly up to touch my palm to his.

He ended up grabbing my hand during the high five, and I swear, this is so cliché, so stupid chick lit banal, but I honestly felt a damned jolt go through me when we touched. I think he felt it too because he looked at our hands, scowled for a second before scrutinizing me closely then let my hand go.

His honey-brown eyes stared in thought into my green ones for a moment before that sexy grin hit his gorgeous face again. "Well, Miss Priss, I might be seeing you around."

"I'll be waiting breathlessly until that moment." At my sarcasm, he grinned again. I rolled my eyes and said, "So… thanks for the help." I'm pretty sure he heard the muttered, "Jerk" I tacked on, but to his credit he didn't say anything as I closed the trunk and rounded the car to get inside, but before I could pull my door closed he was there holding it open.

"You go to Hallervan?" he'd leaned down and asked, and, God, those eyes, that face… that body. My lord he was hot.

"Starting this semester," I answered still trying to pull my door closed.

"Maybe you'll get lucky and see me." He winked then walked away.

"One can only hope," I'd mumbled, rolling my eyes again, before closing my door and driving away.

It was then I looked down and saw my ruined outfit and sandals only then remembering I had an old pair of Keds and a raincoat under the passenger seat. Great.

First Semester: First Week

  I was excited for school, ready to pursue my dream of becoming a journalist. I'd played a year of basketball at Southwest Idaho University, but I'd won a coveted scholarship that would pay for a huge hunk of the cost to attend Hallervan (which had a better journalism department) the next three years, so Dad couldn't complain too much about my wanting to go here. He'd been proud of me but had also been worried because Seattle was a good twelve and a half hours away from the small town of Stone Springs, Idaho, where I'd grown up. But one of my brothers had helped with that since he was attending law school in Moscow, Idaho, which was clear across the state from our hometown, and he'd told Dad that he'd only be five hours from me and that had finalized it. Kind of. Dad had still made me promise to check in with him on a regular basis. I'd agreed because I loved my dad and also because my family was close and I couldn't imagine not talking to any of them at least every few weeks.

  My brothers were four and seven years older than I was, which made me the baby, hence Dad's reluctance to let me go. Heath was the oldest, (his full name was actually Heathcliff) my other brother was Holden and I was Scout. As you probably gathered, our mother had been an avid reader and named us after her favorite literary characters. I'd never known her because she'd died when I was three but I'd always felt her absence in our lives due to all the pictures of her in our house and especially when Dad or one of my brothers brought her up, sharing stories of times I'd never known or didn't remember. When I was seven, I'd asked my dad why he'd never remarried. He'd gotten a faraway look in his eyes and told me that once you found your reason to breathe, no one else could "pass muster." I hadn't understood at the time, but it sounded romantic, so I'd let it go.

  So, back to our names. Although I thought they were cool, Heath despised his, even though his broody spells said the name fit him perfectly. But he'd taken a lot of crap from the other kids for it when he was little, so when I was old enough to know what it meant, I told him his name sounded prestigious and it would look great on business cards someday. He'd laughed at that saying he hoped that all the hell he'd gotten for it would eventually pay off. He was now a software developer in Boise, a job for which he was getting paid bank, so I'd say he'd more than vindicated himself for being picked on. Matter of fact, he was making so much money, he even co-signed for a loan with Dad for our farm. Dad, of course, had balked, but Heath had insisted, telling Dad the money would likely just go to more beer, so Dad had half-jokingly given in for the sake of Heath's sobriety. My other brother Holden, who lived up to his namesake in the fact that he was a deep thinker (and also quite the party boy), was twenty-four, a huge ladies man and was the one in law school who'd convinced Dad to let me come to Seattle. And I'm Scout. I think I've done a decent job living up to my name because I've always been a tomboy and Dad says I've also always been fairly precocious.

So there I sat in psychology class on the first day, when to my utter shock (and annoyance), Tire Change Dude walked in. And, damn it, he was even better looking out of the rain.

He had on a gray short-sleeved Godsmack t-shirt over a long-sleeved black tee, hiding the full sleeves of tattoos that I knew he had, but I could still see part of a tattoo peeking out at the left side of his neck. I saw that his hair was actually a dark caramel-color, not quite as dark as the rain had made it appear, and he wore it in a fade cut with long bangs spiked up in the front. His faded jeans sat low on his hips and he wore brown, lace-up boots. He also had on black reading glasses, and jumping Jesus on a pogo stick, he looked good.

I immediately turned my head away, scratching myself on the neck nonchalantly, hoping he wouldn't recognize me. I then heard a guy several rows behind and a few seats to the left of me holler "Yo!" and I turned slightly to see Tattoo Dude raise his head in a nod at him then he came up the stairs and passed right by me and, damn it, I couldn't *not* look. His eyes caught mine but they looked right through me, no recognition in them at all, which I oddly found was kind of disappointing.

As I sat waiting for class to begin, I listened to the two guys talking and, boy, did I learn a lot. First of all, tire dude's name was Gable. I hadn't remembered what his girlfriend had called him that day in the rain, but now it clicked. Secondly, I found out they'd had a party the weekend before and Gable had gotten so wasted that he'd woken up in bed with three girls, so I guessed the classy babe with him when I had a flat wasn't his girlfriend after all. Thirdly, I now knew he was thinking of getting another tattoo, probably "Luctor et emergo" on his right pec, which I knew was Latin but had no clue what it meant. The guy with him was just as clueless, asking about it, but Gable had remained close-mouthed. Fourthly, their poker game had been changed from Wednesday night to Thursday. And fifthly, who the fuck was the hot blonde piece of tail sitting in front of him with legs that went on for miles that he wouldn't mind having wrapped around his head?

He had to be kidding. Who said stuff like that in public? And did he really think that'd land him a girl? Wow. I inspected the classroom for the poor blond girl he was talking so rudely about, but most of the girls I saw had dark hair. Then I felt something hit the side of my head, and frowning, turned to see him and his friend ogling me as the wadded paper one of them had thrown landed in my lap.

The friend jerked his chin up at me. "What's up? Hey, did you fall from the sky because let's have sex."

I stared at him for a moment before scrunching up my face and saying, "Seriously?" Really, who talked that way?

Gable's eyes narrowed then. "I know you." I squinted my eyes right back at him then he snapped his fingers and pointed at me. "Tire girl. Miss Priss." And he gave me that lopsided grin.

I rolled my eyes and turned away because I was embarrassed by the whole encounter. I was also flustered at the fact that my heart was beating ninety-to-nothing and my nipples had gotten hard at just seeing him grin at me. God.

The professor had now come in and started taking roll, so I kept my attention on her, ignoring the fact that I could feel Gable's eyes burning a hole into the side of my head. I wanted to turn to him and frown, maybe even give him the finger, but I knew that'd just get me another nipple-hardening grin so I stayed facing forward. But as I sat there, using every ounce of restraint I could to keep from looking at him, I realized I was actually flattered by what he'd said about me, and it horrified me that I'd feel that way about being objectified and I wanted to smack myself in the head as I tried figuring out where my self-respect had gone.

During roll call, I learned that his last name was Powers. Oh, boy, he was one of *them*. The *them* I'd been hearing about since stepping onto campus. And he was flirting with me. Well, wasn't I the lucky one. Unable to help being curious about this latest bit of info and wanting to know if he really was as good looking as everyone had been saying (I mean, I'd seen him but hadn't known who he was so I hadn't really *seen him seen him*), I risked a glance over my left shoulder at him only to find him gazing right back at me with a lazy grin. Holy crap! I turned around quickly and promptly swallowed my gum on the breath I'd sucked in at getting caught. As I choked out a cough, I decided he *was* as hot as everyone had been saying, and I also decided I was an idiot to mess with him. Although very handsome, he was uncouth, rude and too wild for the likes of me and I needed to stay far, far away from him, which I told myself I'd do.

So why the hell did that make him even more intriguing?

~*~*~*~

Class finally ended with the professor stating that she was going to have us participate in an experiment which had us being pen pals with another psychology student from any of her classes, all in the name of science. She said the experiment was to see if our emails boosted the other person's academic performance because we were to be encouraging when we wrote. We were not to tell who we were or give too much personal information about ourselves and at the end of the semester we'd be revealed to each other then we'd write a thesis over our experience. She'd posted our student ID numbers on the wall and who we were matched up with, and on our way out, we were to write down the number then email our person that day if possible.

This sounded like fun and since I knew no one in Seattle other than Amy, I hoped I might be able to make a friend for the semester at least. As I stood waiting for the crowd to dissipate, I felt someone right behind me, and it was like my body knew it was him. My breathing instantly sped up, my heart started thumping hard in my chest and I could feel the hair on the back of my neck rise.

"Good to see you again, Priss,"Gable leaned down and whispered into my ear, his hot breath on my neck making me shiver, and, of course, my nipples get rock hard.

Good lord. I'd never experienced a reaction to a guy like this before. I closed my eyes for a moment, wanting to lean my head back against his hard chest and beg him to talk more, to say anything, or maybe nothing as long he stayed close so I could feel him against me, feel the heat that seemed to radiate from him burning into my skin. Instead, I said breathlessly, "My name's not Priss," and heard him chuckle softly, his mouth still at my ear.

"I miss the white outfit," he stated then put his hands on my hips, moving them down to where his fingers skimmed along the hem of my shorts then started moving them slowly back toward my bottom. "But these hot pink shorts make you look completely fuckable too."

That brought me out of my stupor and I spun around, glaring up at him. "You can't talk to me like that!" I hissed under my breath, glancing around self-consciously to make sure no one was watching our exchange.

He peered down at my chest where my nipples were standing at full attention under my t-shirt. "From the looks of it, I think you like me talking to you like that." Then he leaned in closer. "What's the matter? Never been talked dirty to before, Priss?" When he pulled back, I saw that the half grin was now going strong and his luminous brown eyes were dancing with humor at his having riled me.

Holy hell.

As I kept glowering at him, having no response to that, I noticed a girl next to us gawking at us, and embarrassed, I smiled shyly at her, tucking a piece of hair behind my ear, trying to act normal. When she turned away, I whisper-hissed at him, "Are you kidding me right now? Just who do you think you are?"

He bent again to get close to my ear. "I'm the guy who'll have you coming hard before the semester's over," he answered evenly, his eyes shimmering with cockiness as they burned into mine when he stood straight again.

Mesmerized, I gazed back at him, lost in him, wanting what he was selling, God, how did he do that, until it hit me that I should be offended by his boldness and I suddenly frowned. "What is your deal?" I screeched making several students look at me and felt my face burning even hotter than it already was at his inappropriate comments. I turned to get away from him mumbling, "Oh, my God," but he grabbed me by the arm pulling me in close.

"You don't have to call me God. Gable works, but I'm sure I'll be making you scream both soon," he whispered close to my ear.

I pushed against his chest (of course he didn't budge at all) and jerked my arm from his grasp with a scowl then moved as far away from him as I could, going to the back of the line to wait until he left. Standing there, I closed my eyes trying to get a hold of myself but could still see his seductive gaze searing into mine as he smirked while saying those things to me, as if he was so confident that they'd happen regardless of what I had to say about it.

And the really bad thing about it? As I stood there, a complete emotional mess from what'd just happened, I found I actually wanted those things to happen, which served to embarrass me even more not to mention just totally baffle me. I mean, I'd only slept with one guy, Hayden, my first and only boyfriend, and that'd been after we'd dated for almost a year so it wasn't like I got around much, so what was wrong with me that I was all in for having sex with someone I barely knew? Someone who'd been an ass to me from day one. Someone who obviously had way more experience than I had.

As I stood behind everyone, I swallowed thickly, my cheeks still on fire, wondering who the hell I was, and when I moved my eyes to the front I saw Gable write his person's number down in his notebook, smile at a girl who was gazing up at him like he was a damned rock star then he left without even a glance back at me.

When I finally got to the front, I wrote my person's number down quickly and got the heck out of there because a few people were still watching me curiously. As I walked outside the building, I cautiously surveyed the area making sure Gable hadn't hung around wanting to torment me some more but saw that he was off to my right talking to his friend, Mr. Tactful, and they were near the parking lot which was a good twenty yards away. I also saw that Gable was smoking. Well, total turnoff right there. Good. At least he had something about him that repulsed me (other than his cocky attitude, that is), and when I saw the coast was clear, I let out the breath I was holding, relief flooding over me along with a bit of disappointment at his unhealthy habit, and headed away in the opposite direction from him, going to my next class.

~*~*~*~

From: 9565876 <student.9565876@hallervan.edu>

Subject: Hi!

Date: August 28, 3:32 p.m.

Hi 9543254!

It's nice meeting you!

Um, to tell you a few things about myself, I'm a sophomore and female. I'm not from Washington State. I've got two older brothers, and was raised by my dad. My mom died of cancer when I was three, so I was raised by three guys so I guess I'm kind of a tomboy. I love chicken tacos, Alter Bridge is my favorite band (Mark Tremonti is THE best guitarist ever) and I have a huge crush on Alex Trebek. Weird, I know.

I hope your week has gone well so far. How are your classes going? Great, I hope! Mine are going fine. I know we're not supposed to tell each other anything too personal, but I have to tell you, I'm already loving my French class, well, except for when the professor called on us to see how much we knew and I accidentally asked if the chicken was in my size. I was going for sweater, but as you see, I screwed that up.

Anyway, I hope this assignment is fun. I've never had a pen pal before, but if it gets me an A in psych, then I'm in lol

Talk to you later! :)

9565876

My pen pal answered that night.

From: 9543254 <student.9543254@hallervan.edu>

Subject: Hi!

Date: August 28, 10:36 p.m.

To: 9565876 <student.9565876@hallervan.edu>

Yo 9565876—

I'm a dude from the Seattle area. I've got 3 brothers. Jimi Hendrix, enough said. Not much of an Alter Bridge fan, although I haven't really listened to them. Tremonti was good when he was with Creed, though. Chicken tacos are cool. You're into older game show hosts—nice. My classes are good.

What do you look like?

---9543254

~*~*~*~

"How'd it go?" Amy asked when she came in that night from the fast-food place where she worked. She still wore her work uniform that consisted of khaki pants and a crazy colorful striped shirt. She hated it but I thought she looked cute in it and couldn't help smiling at her every time I saw her wearing it which always made her scowl at me. She was about the same height I was but a little thicker since she'd been a gymnast for most of her life, so she was like a walking muscle. Her skin was gorgeous, the color of coffee with cream, and her eyes were a startling sea foam green. She wore her dark brown hair short, similar to Halle Berry's, and I thought she was beautiful.

"Good. How about you?" I was sitting at the kitchen table working on a paper for poli-sci.

"Okay. I've already got a paper due Friday in my advanced comp class. There goes summer." She rolled her eyes and plopped down on the couch, picking up the remote and clicking through channels on the TV like crazy.

I chuckled. "They don't waste time, that's for sure. I'm working on a paper right now."

"What's your topic?" she asked, peeking over the back of the couch at me.

"We have to read something about the American Dream and argue how it impacts different ethnic groups."

"Yawn," she answered. "Ours is something about Hamlet and self-awareness and its meaning. Double yawn."

I chuckled again. "Good times."

"Yeah," she muttered turning back to the TV.

"Hey, do you know a guy named Gable Powers?"

Her head whipped around. "*Everyone* knows who Gable Powers is. Why?"

"Remember the guy who helped me with my flat when I came to meet you?"

"Nuh uh!" she answered, staring at me in disbelief, her mouth hanging open.

I rolled my eyes and nodded. "Yeah, and now he's in my psych class and is just as big a jerk as he was the first time I met him."

"He's hot, Scout."

"He might be hot, but after today, I know he's still a jerk."

"What happened?"

I told her what he'd said and she squealed. "Holy shit! He wants you!"

"Maybe in a Cro-Magnon sort of way."

She laughed. "Still," she said grinning at me, wiggling her eyebrows, which made me snort. "Keep me posted on what else he says." She turned back to the TV and I frowned, not having thought that he and I would have another encounter.

"God, I was hoping that was it…" I mumbled.

"From the way it sounds, I don't think it's over," she said as she continued turning from one station to the next with the remote. I bit my lip and frowned, staring at my laptop and wondering what else he might have to say to me. "Okay, on that, I'm gonna take a shower," she said as she stood, muttering on her way out of the living room that she couldn't take smelling like a giant French fry any longer which brought me out of my ruminating and made me chuckle.

I'd lucked out that Amy was a good roommate. I'd been a little wary because Heath and Holden had told me some scary stories about their former roomies, but thank God that wasn't the case for me.

Week Two

From: 9565876 <student.9565876@hallervan.edu>

Subject: Hello =)

Date: September 3, 8:03 a.m.

To: 9543254 <student.9543254@hallervan.edu>

Dear 9543254,

What do I look like... I'm about 5'7" and weigh around 125. I have long, blond hair and green eyes. How about you?

You only have brothers too?

I agree that Hendrix was probably the best, though I'd say Tremonti is a close second :)

Seattle has produced some amazing musicians and bands. You're lucky to have grown up here if you like music.

I hope you're enjoying your 2nd week at Hallervan.

I think French class is going to kick my ass.

Talk to you later,

9565876

From: 9543254 <student.9543254@hallervan.edu>

Subject: Hello =)

Date: September 4, 5:49 p.m.

To: 9565876 <student.9565876@hallervan.edu>

Six,

You sound hot. Are you hot?

I'm 6'2" with brown hair and eyes and I have tattoos. You have any tattoos?

Yep. 3 brothers. I'm 2nd oldest.

Nirvana. Pearl Jam. Alice in Chains. Seattle is the Mecca of all things grunge.

School's cool. Sorry about French.

~*~*~*~

Monday after class, I applied at a couple places for a job because I needed the extra cash. Dad was giving me money for gas and groceries, but I wanted to help some too, so I'd made the rounds around town, going in and filling out applications then coming home and filling out others on my laptop. I'd already gotten a call from a sports bar at which I'd applied and they'd scheduled me to come in Wednesday for an interview.

I also applied for the campus newspaper and was "hired" to review movies, which was the start to my journalism career. Whoopee! My column would provide a weekly critique of a movie every Friday, giving it one to ten Bulldog paws in honor of Hallervan's mascot. The good thing was, I could review any movie I wanted, not just new ones and since I was a huge movie buff, I was excited about this gig.

I hadn't seen Gable since the first day of psych class, but I hadn't really been looking for him, either. No, let me rephrase that. I *had* been looking for him but only to make sure I avoided him. But I'd seen his friend a few times and had made dang sure not to make eye contact with him.

I sat in the student center on Thursday eating a hamburger for lunch as I reviewed some notes for French when someone said, "You're in my poli-sci class."

Looking up I saw a guy I didn't recognize with a tray of food standing there smiling down at me. "I am?"

He chuckled. "Yeah. You mind?" he asked, nodding at the table.

"Oh, no, go right ahead," I said, clearing my books out of his way and hoping he wasn't a jerk who'd ruin my day.

He set his tray down then pulled out a chair and once seated, held his hand out to me. "Bodhi Matthews."

I shook his hand. "Scout Patterson."

"Scout?"

"Yep." I was used to people repeating my name since it was unusual but it didn't bother me at all because I liked my name.

"Cool." He took a plate of lasagna off his tray along with a piece of lemon meringue pie and a bottle of water. Once he was settled, he lowered his head in prayer and several seconds later dug in.

"So, you're in my class..." I stated having no clue what to say to this guy. He was very tall and slender with curly brown hair and big, blue eyes. The wire-rimmed glasses he wore gave him a somewhat academic, if not nerdy, appearance.

"Yeah," he said, chewing on his food. When he swallowed, he added, "You sit two rows in front of me." He continued scarfing down his food.

"What year are you?"

After several seconds of chewing then taking a drink, he answered, "Junior."

We sat in silence for several minutes. "So where're you from, Bodhi?" Maybe he'd get tired of my questions and leave. I mean, he'd initiated things and there were at least twenty other tables open that he could've sat at but he'd chosen mine, interrupting my study time.

"Coeur d'Alene."

"Really? I'm from Idaho too. Stone Springs. Small town near Idaho Falls."

"Cool."

All righty then. Since our conversation wasn't going very far, I decided to ignore him and continued looking over my French notes.

"So, you like it here?" he finally asked.

"Yeah," I replied, still studying my notes.

"Wanna hang out sometime?"

I glanced up at him and frowned. "Well, you're not the most vociferous person."

He laughed. "Sorry. I was just really hungry. I work the graveyard shift stocking at Walmart and went right to class from there, so I didn't get breakfast."

I nodded, giving him a small smile. He was kind of weird, but I always thought weird was interesting. When he finished his lasagna, he started on his pie, which took about five seconds for him to inhale. Then he downed his water and let out a big sigh.

"Okay, brain's fully functioning now." He grinned. "Let's start over. I'm Bodhi and you're Scout. What's with the name?"

I laughed. "I have the same question about yours. But my mom loved books. *To Kill a Mockingbird* was one of her favorites." I shrugged.

"That's awesome. Well, I'm Bodhi because my parents are Buddhists." I raised an eyebrow at him and he snorted. "I know. Tall, gay, white boy who's a Buddhist." He shrugged. "My parents were hippies. They almost named me Mohandas Karamchand after Ghandi. Thank God, they went for Bodhi. My sister is Dharma Nirvana. She's a junior in high school back home. She and I were both glad Mom and Dad stopped having kids after us. Our next little brother or sister was gonna be named Sanskrit."

I couldn't help but giggle. "You're a funny guy, Bodhi."

"Yeah, well, it's the gay thing."

This made me laugh even more. "Oh, that's bad."

He chuckled and wiped his mouth. "Yeah, I know."

"So what brought you to Hallervan?" I asked.

"My parents went here, so I thought I'd try it." He shrugged. "What brought you here?"

"I won a scholarship to the journalism department, so I took them up on it," I explained. "What's your major?"

"Well, I went back and forth for a while but think I've finally nailed it down—education. High school social studies. So now I'm backtracking some and picking up some classes I missed. What year are you?"

"Sophomore. Oh, good. I might need your help with the paper we were assigned," I informed him with a grin.

"It'd be my honor." He smiled widely. I liked this guy. "Well, it was nice meeting you, Scout. *Now* do you wanna hang out sometime?" he asked, putting all his trash on his tray.

I smiled back at him. "Sure. Maybe you can teach me how to be more zen."

"I can do that. 'Kay, I'll see you tomorrow in class," he said still smiling as he stood, picking up his tray before leaving.

I smiled for a long time after he left knowing I'd just made a new friend which was awesome.

Week Three

From: 9565876 <student.9565876@hallervan.edu>

Subject: Me again!

Date: September 9, 7:54 a.m.

To: 9543254 <student.9543254@hallervan.edu>

Hey (should I call you Four since you called me by the last number in my ID?)

Am I hot? Hm. My ex-boyfriend used to say I was, so maybe? How about you? Are you hot? lol

No, no tattoos, but if I did get one, I'd probably have, "He gave us two soap dolls, a broken watch and chain, a pair of good-luck pennies, and our lives..." put on the back of my right shoulder. Silly, I know.

Also are you athletic? I was an All-Idaho basketball player and played one year in college but I won a big scholarship here, so I decided to use it instead.

You're a middle child, huh? Does that mean you're the black sheep? ;) I'm the baby and my older brothers are very protective. I've only had one boyfriend and they had him so scared at first, it's a wonder he stuck around.

Don't forget Foo Fighters and Heart.

Thanks. I think my goal of a 4.0 can kiss itself goodbye because of French.

I hope you're still liking your classes!

See ya!

From: 9543254 <student.9543254@hallervan.edu>

Subject: Me again!

Date: September 4, 5:49 p.m.

To: 9565876 <student.9565876@hallervan.edu>

You can call me whatever you want, Six.

Ever know of a guy who doesn't think he's hot?

All-State football player but blew out my knee in the championship game senior year. Quarterback. Had scholarships too but lost them because of my knee, so I decided to follow my brother here. My two younger brothers are here also.

To Kill a Mockingbird, huh? Favorite book?

Yeah, I'm the big screw-up black sheep. Haven't declared a major. Always getting in trouble. My brothers fuck with me about it all the time. Bastards. But I love them.

Classes are good. Maybe I'll have a major figured out soon…

All three of his brothers went here.

Holy shit.

Was my pen pal Gable? Oh, God, please, no.

But several things matched up to what I knew of him so far: My pen pal was cocky. He had three brothers. Tattoos. Who else could it be? Time to put my investigative instincts to work and find out. Then I'd have a little talk with my psychology professor and see if she could change us if it really was him.

~*~*~*~

I got the job at O'Leary's Sports Bar and Grill and started training the next week. I'd worked as a waitress at Rosie's Country Kitchen when I was in high school, so I was familiar with this type of job, and I already kind of knew the ropes, so I hoped to pick things up quickly.

A girl named Alyssa was my trainer and she was kind of a bitch, but whatever. I followed her around for an hour thinking my only problem would be memorizing the menu, but I knew that would eventually come.

"And after your shift is over, you have to roll silverware and fill salt and pepper shakers. If you don't, Jack will dock your pay so you'd better make sure you're paying attention," she said after my training was over and rolled her big, blue eyes at me as if I'd been a huge inconvenience to her before she flipped her long, brown hair over her shoulder and walked off to check on a table.

"Don't mind her. She's been stuck in bitch mode ever since one of the bartenders blew her off. She's got the hots for him, but there's no way she's special enough to land him. I'm Natalie by the way." She was another waitress and she gave me a gorgeous smile. She was tall and had short, brown hair that hit her at the shoulders, and her brown eyes had twinkled when she'd given me the info about Alyssa. I liked Natalie right away.

"Hey, Natalie. I'm Scout. Thanks for that. I thought she just didn't like me," I said with a chuckle.

She laughed. "She doesn't like anyone who can't do something for her. But she's a good waitress. I'm sure you've seen her fakeness in action all night."

I snickered. "Well, I wasn't sure, but at least it got her some good tips."

I left thirty minutes later after rolling silverware with Alyssa who griped the entire time about the bartender she was dating who'd stood her up for a poker game. By the time I got home, I was ready for some silence.

Week Four

From: 9565876 <student.9565876@hallervan.edu>

Subject: Trouble-making screw-up

Date: September 18, 10:39 p.m.

To: 9543254 <student.9543254@hallervan.edu>

Hi,

Sorry to hear about your knee. That sucks. Do you have a favorite quarterback?

To Kill a Mockingbird is definitely a favorite.

Black sheep, huh? Been to jail? Busted for drugs? Broken any hearts?

My family's really close. My dad's a farmer and we all helped out. I could drive a tractor by the time I was 7.

What's your biggest goal in life?

Talk to you later

From: 9543254 <student.9543254@hallervan.edu>

Subject: Trouble-making screw-up

Date: September 18, 11:02 p.m.

To: 9565876 <student.9565876@hallervan.edu>

Thanks. Yeah, it did suck. Two of my brothers play sports in college and it's sometimes tough watching them play when I want to be out there too. But I'm glad they're getting to live the dream. My youngest brother was a good athlete too but he's more of a computer geek, so he doesn't play sports anymore.

Steve Young was my favorite QB.

Yes. Yes. No. Yes.

My family's pretty close too although we try to stay out of each other's business most of the time. Mom runs a daycare and Dad works as a mechanic, so yes, I know how to change a diaper and oil.

Damn. Driving a tractor at age 7? That's pretty badass. Ever wreck? ;)

My biggest goal in life is to be happy. And while I'm at it, if I make others happy, that'd be good too.

What's yours?

xx

I was lying in bed when my phone dinged. When I looked at it, I was surprised to see that he'd answered back so quickly. I read through what he'd written and when I got to the bottom, I stared at the two X's. If I wasn't mistaken, they stood for kisses. He was sending me virtual kisses now? Yesterday, I'd asked one of the guys who worked for the newspaper who was pretty computer savvy if he could access student files and he was checking into whether this was Gable or not. If this really was him, at least I now knew he had a sweet side.

After reading his responses I was curious so I wrote him back right away.

From: 9565876 <student.9565876@hallervan.edu>

Subject: Trouble-making screw-up

Date: September 18, 11:07 p.m.

To: 9543254 <student.9543254@hallervan.edu>

So, for clarity's sake:

Yes, you're the black sheep.

Yes, you've been to jail.

No, you've never been arrested for drugs.

Yes, you've broken hearts.

Did I get that right?

No wrecks on the tractor although I did back my brother against a barbed-wire fence with it and held him there for ten minutes because he kept teasing me about a boy in my class when I was 11. He never teased me about boys again.

Those are some very nice goals. Mine? To get as much information to the people that I can even if it means stepping on toes. What can I say? I'm a fighter for the rights of people everywhere =) And I'm pretty sure it'll make me happy, and I hope others will be happy too because they'll be well-informed.

xo

Oh, God. I didn't know if I should leave exes and ohs or not, but I decided to go with it, cringing a bit when I hit "Send." I guess I'd see whether I'd made a colossal mistake when he wrote back. And that he did a few minutes later.

From: 9543254 <student.9543254@hallervan.edu>

Subject: Trouble-making screw-up

Date: September 18, 11:13 p.m.

To: 9565876 <student.9565876@hallervan.edu>

Black sheep, yes.

Jail, yes.

Drugs, no.

Broken hearts? Yes. Lots. Not bragging, but I've had a lot of girlfriends, and by a lot, I mean, a lot. Does that intimidate you? Have you only had the one boyfriend? Just curious.

And just as I thought. You're badass...

xx

Wow. He was being so open about everything, so I thought I'd strike while the iron was hot.

From: 9565876 <student.9565876@hallervan.edu>

Subject: Trouble-making screw-up

Date: September 18, 11:20 p.m.

To: 9543254 <student.9543254@hallervan.edu>

What makes you the black sheep?

Jail? Care to explain? Lol

Good on no drugs.

A lot, huh? Are we talking double digits? Triple? How many is a lot? 20? And you've broken all their hearts?

Have you ever had your heart broken?

Yes, only one "real" boyfriend. We dated for two years, but after graduating high school two years ago, he went to Johns Hopkins pre-med and I went to college closer to home. We tried the long-distance thing, but had to call it quits after six months. It was too hard keeping up with each other. Besides, he was two hours ahead in Baltimore, so that made it tough to even talk by phone because he was always tired from studying. So when it was ten my time, it was midnight there so we rarely connected. Now here comes the hard part of it all. Even though I'd planned on breaking up with him, it wasn't until after I found out that he and my best friend had been "talking" (which is code for screwing like rabbits) for over a year that we did. I was so hurt. I mean, our relationship had pretty much run its course, so it wasn't really that. It was just the betrayal of it all that got me the most. I've had some trust issues ever since. I'm sure you can understand.

The thing that really pissed me off about it all was when I found out and confronted him on the phone, he tried telling me he was "fucked up" and that I should've stayed away from the start. I had no idea what that meant, other than it was just an excuse for his being a cheating scumbag. God, such a copout.

But, yeah, I not only lost a boyfriend, I lost my best friend of thirteen years too, which was what really sucked. I've dated a couple guys over the last year but nothing serious...

Have you ever been serious with a girl?

xo

From: 9543254 <student.9543254@hallervan.edu>

Subject: Trouble-making screw-up

Date: September 18, 11:23 p.m.

To: 9565876 <student.9565876@hallervan.edu>

I'm the black sheep because I'm a hellraiser (according to my oldest brother).

Jail for DUI my sophomore year in high school, breaking and entering (a friend and I broke into our high school just to be dicks), and possession of stolen property (jealous ex had given me an old iPhone of hers then called the cops when I'd broken it off with her saying I stole it. I gave it back, charges were dropped, I spread a rumor that she had herpes, all was well. Hey, I was sixteen).

A lot. Hm. If I told you it was over 30 would you think bad of me?

Your ex sounds like a fucking prick and your friend sounds like a cunt. They deserve each other's fucked up selves.

Yes. I've had my heart broken. Yes, I was serious with her. Not sure I want to talk about it.

So are you a virgin?

xx

Uh. Wow. That escalated quickly.

Did I really want to talk to him about this? He'd been pretty open with me and it was way too easy telling him things behind an email address. I guessed it couldn't hurt anything since I'd have our professor change our pen pals if this really was Gable, so he'd never know it was me anyway.

From: 9565876 <student.9565876@hallervan.edu>

Subject: Trouble-making screw-up

Date: September 18, 11:30 p.m.

To: 9543254 <student.9543254@hallervan.edu>

You sound a lot like my middle brother. I guess he was a hellraiser too. He almost got a DUI his jr year in hs, but since my dad was good friends with the sheriff, he talked him out of it telling him he'd put my brother to work. And he did. My brother was grounded almost all summer and worked his ass off on the farm. He's a heartbreaker too. I think he had at least 50 girlfriends during hs or it seemed that way.

Why does it matter if I think badly of you? You can talk about anything you want with me. I won't judge. But only if you're comfortable.

And thanks. They're definitely not my two favorite people by a long shot.

No, I'm not a virgin, but my ex has been my one and only. I guess I'm old school because I think you need to care about each other before you take that step. That's pretty lame, huh?

xo

From: 9543254 <student.9543254@hallervan.edu>

Subject: Trouble-making screw-up

Date: September 18, 11:34 p.m.

To: 9565876 <student.9565876@hallervan.edu>

Not lame at all. I agree that it's much better when you have feelings for the other person. But as a guy, well, you've got brothers, so I'm sure you understand somewhat that it's just different. Not sure how to explain it. It just is. Call me sexist if you want. I mean, if I had a sister, I'd kick a guy's teeth in if he even tried touching her. Weird, right?

I don't know why it matters if you think bad of me. It just does.

I'm glad you don't.

xx

> Hi Sexist,
>
> How are you?
>
> xo

> Funny.
>
> xx

I left it at that. I had class in the morning so I needed sleep and just as I was drifting off, my phone dinged again.

> I'm glad I have you to talk to... thanks for listening. You might be the first chick I've ever been just friends with.

xx

Oh, wow. Now what was I going to do with this? Gable really did have a sweet side (if this was actually him). I took a deep breath and blew it out knowing if he kept being nice, it might spell out trouble for me. I mean, I was already wildly attracted to him physically, but if on top of that he turned out to be a decent human being, I knew I'd be in danger of possibly falling in serious like with him. Definitely needed to be careful here.

From: 9565876 <student.9565876@hallervan.edu>

Subject: Thanks

Date: September 19, 12:13 a.m.

To: 9543254 <student.9543254@hallervan.edu>

I'm glad you're glad ;) I'm glad too.

Goodnight

xo

I closed my eyes and smiled that he might not be as bad as I thought he was.

Boy, was I wrong.

Week Five

I'd finished my training at O'Leary's, gotten my permit to serve alcohol and had been on my own for a week now. I'd only worked short shifts from five to seven, but tonight I was on the clock until eleven. It was Monday, but working that late wasn't too bad because my apartment was only about ten minutes away, so I'd be home before midnight and my first class wasn't until ten in the morning, so I'd have time to study some for the test I had in French.

Things tonight had been going great so far. I'd made some pretty good tips because NFL football had started and since there were five TVs in the place, it seemed as if every guy in town had shown up to watch and have a couple beers. And if I'd learned anything from working at Rosie's, it was that beer made guys happy and if there was a ballgame on, they were even happier, which meant they tipped well.

So I made my rounds again, grabbing beer mugs and pitchers for refills, making my way to the bar and that was when my night started going not so great.

"Priss! When'd you start working here?"

Oh, God. Gable was a bartender and he was grinning from ear to ear at me. And, damn, did he look good. He had on a football jersey too, but his was a full jersey that he had tucked into the front of his jeans. His hair was styled how he'd worn it in class and he had his glasses on. His tattoos were on full display and my stomach fluttered as I stood looking at him.

"You've got to be shitting me," I finally mumbled, placing my tray of three mugs and two pitchers on the bar. I glanced up at him and gave him my best indifferent face. I liked this job, I'd now memorized the menu and I really didn't want to quit even if he was going to act rudely toward me.

"So… I like the jersey." He kept his grin and nodded at the 49ers half jersey I was wearing. Waitresses' wore half jerseys as their uniform during football season that showed our bellies, and I realized that Gable and I wore the same team and we both had the number forty-nine. Yay. I honestly didn't know anything about pro ball, so I'd just grabbed a couple jerseys when Jack had told me to pick last week. But I thought they were cute and I did have a flat stomach since I'd been an athlete, so although they'd taken a little getting used to at first, I found I really wasn't that self-conscious about them. I also think I got better tips wearing them, so whatever. In December, we'd switch to basketball jerseys which were the full jersey, thank God, then we'd wear baseball jerseys until football began again in the fall.

I smiled weakly at him then told him what each order was, watching as he turned to fill them. Damn. Even his butt was nice. And the way he carried himself, so confident, was freakin' hot.

"Thanks," I murmured after he filled the last pitcher, setting it on the bar. He stood watching me for a moment as I loaded my tray. Irritated with being scrutinized, I glared at him with a scowl. "What?"

He grinned. "Nothing. Just makes everything easier now." I was still scowling when he winked then he turned away to take a customer's order.

Easier? What'd that mean? Was he talking about hooking up with me? Not happening if he was going to be a jackass to me all the time. I didn't care how sweet he was in his emails. Well, I wasn't going to let him bother me. I needed this job so my plan was to just ignore him as best I could.

And it was a good plan until around the third trip I made to the bar.

"I like black," he said waggling his eyebrows at me.

It took me a second to realize he was talking about my bra that I'd made the mistake of wearing because it showed through the little holes in the white jersey's fabric. I gave him a bored look then put the drinks on my tray and walked away.

On the fourth trip, he said, "Like the jeans, Priss." I still gave him no reaction.

Fifth trip, he leaned over the counter and mumbled, "*Really* like those jeans."

By the sixth trip, I'd had it. I'd brought four pitchers and when he'd filled them all, he'd leered at me and said, "How 'bout we add twenty and go for it."

When I'd frowned and seemed puzzled, he'd pointed at my jersey then back to his slowly. When he saw my eyes get big, he'd grinned wickedly. Forty-nine plus twenty equals sixty-nine. What an ass.

"Are you always this immature? What are you, like thirteen?" I stated giving him an apathetic look.

He narrowed his eyes at me and I could tell I'd offended him. Good. "I'm twenty-one," he replied indignantly. I thought he was finished and I was mentally chalking up a tally for myself when he opened his mouth again. "In my prime, sweetheart. Can't wait to prove it to you. Over and over and over."

Despite the fact that my body was now fully alert and reacting to what he'd said, butterflies in my stomach going nuts and nipples all freaking perky, damn it, I gritted my teeth and snapped, "You do know there's a thing called sexual harassment?" I glared at him then added, "And don't call me sweetheart."

He snorted. "Go ahead and report me. What have I said that can be construed as anything sexual? You may have taken it that way, but to me, it was pretty innocent." He then smiled impishly.

I frowned and thought of the things he'd said and he was right. It was all pretty innocent on the surface; I was just inferring that what he was saying was sexual. Crap.

"Besides, Jack's my uncle. I'm his favorite nephew. He knows I wouldn't do anything like that." He shrugged and the damned smirk he sported was begging to be slapped right off his beautiful face. He wiped his hands with a small towel and threw it to the side then crossed his arms over his chest, leaning back against the counter. As I picked up my tray and started to walk away, he tacked on, "Or you could just quit." I turned back to see him watching me, his eyes challenging, daring.

"Wh—what?" I sputtered. I'd never quit anything in my life. It wasn't how I was raised. As he stared at me with that damned smug expression, I finally gave him a scowl then turned and headed to my tables knowing there was no way I was quitting now. Stubbornness was in every Patterson's blood. And also a competitive nature. And bullheadedness. Nope. Not quitting.

So stupid, stupid me sucked it up, knowing I'd never be the first to wave the white flag. Fantastic.

~*~*~*~

My shift was almost over so I was rolling silverware in the back. Alyssa had the night off but came in to get her paycheck and had been her usual charming self, giving me a snotty look as she'd walked through to the office to talk to Jack which made me roll my eyes. I'd gone to the back to complete the innocuous little chore and had noticed that Gable hadn't been at the bar so I assumed either his shift was over or he was on break.

"Hey, take this out to the back, would you?" Glen, one of the kitchen guys, asked, handing me a box of slimy, wilted vegetable leftovers.

"Sure," I muttered, grabbing the nasty thing from him and heading out the back door into the alley. As I walked to the Dumpster, I heard giggling and turned to see Gable, who had Alyssa pinned against the back wall of the bar and I froze.

"That tickles!" she said with another giggle as he nibbled on her neck.

"Mmm, you taste good," he mumbled, pulling his head away but keeping his hands against the wall on either side of her face, his hips pinned against hers. I must've let out a gasp because he suddenly turned his head toward me then smirked when he saw what I knew was a whole lot of astonishment on my face.

Startled out of my reverie, I said, "Just taking out the trash! Didn't mean to interrupt." My face burned as I opened the lid to the Dumpster and threw the box inside.

"Like the show, Priss? Jealous?" he asked when I turned around, which made Alyssa giggle some more.

I shot a look at him as I walked back to the door. "Can you for once not be a jerk?" As I grabbed the doorknob, I glared at him and added, "Why is that so hard?"

"That's what she said," he answered with a snort and a leer before turning back to Alyssa who was now laughing like some damned hyena but stopped when he pressed his mouth to hers and kissed her hard.

Ugh.

Why did seeing that make me want to throw up (other than the fact that she was a heinous bitch and he was a complete douche)? I went back inside quickly, washed my hands and finished rolling up my silverware. A few minutes later Alyssa came in, her hair appropriately mussed, and gave me a smug look. She flirted with Glen on her way through, doing her hyena laugh again when he flirted right back, which made me want to punch a puppy. A moment later, Gable came in, walking through as if I didn't exist, nodding his head at Glen before going back out to the bar. It wasn't lost on me that he'd probably had to stay out there longer to adjust himself from being aroused. God.

When I finished with the silverware, I clocked out then left through the back, not wanting to walk through the place and see Alyssa and Gable flirting or in another heated lip lock, or hell, she could've been on her knees behind the fucking bar giving him head for all I knew. When I got in my car, I slammed the door, started it and peeled out of the parking lot then headed to my apartment.

And, man, I was so fucking angry! And what made me even madder was I didn't know if I was more pissed at myself that I'd let what I'd seen affect me or that I was infuriated at Gable for flirting with me all night long then turning around and acting like such a prick.

But you know what? Why the hell did I care? He was nothing to me. *Nothing.* If he wanted to make out with rude bitches that was his business not mine. I'd known he was bad news from the start, so this was all on me because stupid me had to get all caught up in the fact that he may have had a nice side. Well, fuck him. I was *so* over Gable Powers and I was moving on and never looking back because, and I repeat, he meant nothing to me.

So why did this hurt so bad?

~*~*~*~

When I got home, Amy was already asleep, so after I showered then went to bed, I lay there in the dark and got even more pissed off about what'd happened. God! I'd been so humiliated at catching them back there. It'd just been so... gross.

As I lay there stewing over everything, I suddenly sat up and sucked in a deep breath at my discovery, totally wanting to scream because it finally came to me that my problem wasn't that I was repulsed at catching them making out or even that I was disgusted that he'd embarrassed me.

No, I was pissed because I realized that I *was* jealous and wished it'd been *me* out there with him instead of Alyssa.

Oh, my God.

It was times like this that I wished that Ivy and I were still best friends. She would've understood what was going on and told me what to do. But she was in Baltimore with my ex-boyfriend, going pre-med too, just as they'd planned behind my back. The last I'd heard, they were going to get an apartment together and live out the dream. Whatever.

So, feeling lost, I grabbed my phone and shot off an email to my pen pal who may or may not have been the prick I was upset over.

From: 9565876 <student.9565876@hallervan.edu>

Subject: Pissed off

Date: September 24, 12:15 a.m.

To: 9543254 <student.9543254@hallervan.edu>

Ever have nights where you wanted to strangle someone?

From: 9543254 <student.9543254@hallervan.edu>

Subject: Pissed off

Date: September 24, 12:20 a.m.

To: 9565876 <student.9565876@hallervan.edu>

Yep. All the fucking time. What's up?

From: 9565876 <student.9565876@hallervan.edu>

Subject: Pissed off

Date: September 24, 12:22 a.m.

To: 9543254 <student.9543254@hallervan.edu>

Just a guy I know. Why does everything have to be so hard?

From: 9543254 <student.9543254@hallervan.edu>

Subject: Pissed off

Date: September 24, 12:24 a.m.

To: 9565876 <student.9565876@hallervan.edu>

Six... you're makin' this too easy...

That's what she said... ;)

And I knew right then it *had* to be him. Bastard.

Week Six

From: 9543254 <student.9543254@hallervan.edu>

Subject: You there?

Date: October 1, 9:54 p.m.

To: 9565876 <student.9565876@hallervan.edu>

Six,

You okay?

xx

~*~*~*~

At the beginning of the week, Chris had informed me that my pen pal was indeed one Gable Stephen Powers, and I wasn't quite sure what to do—go to Dr. Horner and ask to be switched, or ride it out. I'd talked to Amy about it (not telling her about the lovely revelation I'd had about how I'd wished he'd been making out with me instead of Alyssa, of course) and she'd advised me to give it a week, telling me that if he was rude either in person or through email, then I should ask to be changed. So even though I was giving it another chance, that still didn't mean I was gung-ho to write to him, having not sent anything since the night I'd seen him and Alyssa behind the bar.

~*~*~*~~

On Wednesday morning I got out some paper and a pen to take notes in psychology as Dr. Horner began her lecture.

"Everyone knows Freud is the founding father of psychoanalysis," she began and that was when Gable came in late, walked up the steps, stopped at my row, crossed in front of me and had a seat right next to me.

"Mornin', Priss," he said with a grin as he got out his own paper and pen. He arranged his paper on his desktop then sat there all studiously paying attention to the lecture as if I wasn't there, and all I could do the whole while was sit and fume, wanting to smack his stupid face.

Wow. What an ass.

I finally turned my attention back to the lecture and immediately regretted showing up for class. Jesus, why hadn't I just stayed home in bed?

"Freud believed that our lives consisted of two realms: tension and pleasure. He felt that all tension was grounded in the libido and if it was repressed, depression ensued, meaning, when we deny ourselves sexual pleasure, we can never truly be happy. That's one thing on which my husband agrees with Freud," Dr. Horner said and got a smattering of laughter from the class.

Gable leaned over and whispered, "See, Priss? Let it happen. I'll make you so happy you won't stop smiling for days."

I batted him away and heard him chuckling at me. Douche bag.

"The psychosexual stages of development coincide with our ages, according to Freud. The first stage, ages zero to one, is oral: licking, sucking, swallowing, anything to do with the mouth."

Gable's knee knocked into mine and I gritted my teeth but didn't dare look at him because I knew he'd be donning his nipple-hardening half grin.

Again, why the hell did I show up today?

"Ages one to three years is the anal stage..."

Dear God. I steadfastly focused on my notes and not the idiot who I knew was now grinning from ear-to-ear at my side.

"The phallic stage is where masturbation becomes a new source of pleasure and the Superego develops…"

Gable's hand came over and he started writing on my paper. When he moved it away, my eyes drifted down to see what he'd written. *Would love to watch you masturbate some time, Priss.*

I sucked in a breath upon seeing that, my face flushing as I felt a dip in my freakin' womb which immediately made my panties soaked, fully aware that my nipples had hardened despite my mental protest, as my entire body reacted to his words. Good lord, he was even unsettling using a damned pen.

After forcing myself to relax, underneath what he wrote I penned, *Never gonna happen.*

He reached back and wrote, *It will. You can't resist me.*

I wrote back, *Watch me.*

I heard him chuckling quietly beside me as if resistance were futile or something, like we were living in a *Star Trek* movie or some shit. I just shook my head and kept taking notes, putting him on ignore as best I could, regardless of how many knee knocks he gave me the rest of the time.

When class was dismissed, I turned and glared at him.

"What?" he asked, his lips tipping up.

"Just what do you think you're doing?" I hissed under my breath, so tired of him keeping me off balance with his stupid, sexy self.

"I'll be doing you soon," he responded.

Oh, my God.

"You're a huge jerk," I snapped, shoving my notebook into my bag.

"You're right about me being huge, Priss."

"God, why'd I even come today?" and I knew my mistake the minute I said this.

"I just seem to have that effect on women," he answered, grinning.

I huffed out a laugh. God, he was annoying. "You're too much." I stood and started down the steps.

"That's definitely what she said," he replied from behind me.

This all just pissed me off because, God help me, I was totally into him and I knew he was just messing with me, so once outside, I spun around to face him. "This has to stop now, Gable. You can't talk to me like that."

His eyes danced with amusement then he leaned down and whispered in my ear, "Apparently, I can and you love it. You think I can't see how you respond to me?"

I pulled my face away from him as I took a step back. "That's called disgust."

"It's called lust. You know you want me." His honey eyes burned into mine. I shook my head, throwing in an eye roll, and walked away only to hear him call after me, "As soon as you admit it, things'll be a lot more fun."

That's what I was afraid of.

~*~*~*~

Thursday night I sat at the kitchen table staring at my phone knowing I should just reply to Gable's email and ignore my dumbass feelings for him when Amy came in with a bag of hamburgers and fries from work.

"Hey, thought you might be hungry," she said, setting the bag on the table. A bag whose contents assaulted my nose with all things delicious, that is.

"Just when I think you can't get any better..." I said, reaching a hand in and pulling out a paper-wrapped burger and a carton of fries. "I haven't eaten all day. This smells amazing." I tore open the paper and stuffed my mouth full of glorious, juicy beef. Yum.

Amy laughed. "Calm down, Hoover. You're practically inhaling it."

"I can't help it. So... good..." I answered, mouth full. When I swallowed, I asked, "You're not eating?"

"Already did. And, once again, I smell like a giant French fry and need a shower." She started down the hallway then turned and informed me, "There are two more burgers and fries in there if that one doesn't do the trick."

"'Kay," I mumbled as I chewed, knowing that since the burgers were huge, I wasn't even sure I could finish the one I was munching on. When my phone rang, I saw it was Bodhi calling. "'Lo," I answered as I stuffed some fries into my mouth.

"What's up? Did I interrupt dinner?" He chuckled at hearing my garbled voice.

"Yeah, but it's okay. Amy brought some burgers and fries home from work."

"Some?" he asked, his interest piqued.

I snorted. I'd eaten lunch several more times with him and it was safe to say the guy could seriously throw down some chow. "Got two of everything left. You're more than welcome to them."

"Be there in ten," and he hung up.

I walked down the hallway and knocked on the bathroom door.

"Yeah?" Amy yelled over the shower.

I opened the door and stuck my head inside. "Bodhi's coming over to eat the other burgers. That okay?"

"That's fine. Just make sure to tell his gay ass to stop and get some beer. I've fed him twice already this week."

"Gotcha," I said with a snort, closing the door and going back to the table to get my phone and text him.

Text Message—Thurs, Oct 3, 9:34 p.m.

Me: Amy says to bring beer because she's already fed you twice this week. And she also won't give you her brother's # if you don't.

I threw that last part in just to mess with him.

Text Message—Thurs, Oct 3, 9:34 p.m.

Bodhi: Damn. Tell her to stop being so bossy. And who says I want to meet her brother anyway?

Text Message—Thurs, Oct 3, 9:35 p.m.

Me: Long eye lashes. Hazel eyes. Muscles. Cute butt.

Text Message—Thurs, Oct 3, 9:35 p.m.

Bodhi: Shit. I'll get a case…

This made me laugh out loud.

Bodhi and Amy had met two weeks ago when I'd invited him over to help me with my first movie review and they'd absolutely hit it off by instantly throwing insults at each other. When she'd told him that her older brother who attended UDub was gay and single and that Bodhi was totally his type then shown him some pictures, we both could tell he was interested. I think it may have been the way his mouth had hung open when he'd seen the pictures. Or maybe that he'd grabbed her phone and sent them to his own phone which made Amy warn him that he'd better not be adding them to his spank bank. Bodhi had blushed profusely at that which had made us crack up at him.

While I waited for him to get here, I sat at the table researching a couple movies on my laptop, hoping he'd be willing to help me again. I also once more contemplated emailing Gable but decided to wait until later.

Amy had dressed and come out of her bedroom just in time to answer the door when Bodhi knocked.

"What's up, loser?" she stated upon letting him in.

"Not much, loserette," he countered. He walked into the kitchen, setting the beer he'd bought on the counter then tossed each of us a bottle before putting the rest in the fridge.

"What kinda beer is this?" Amy asked examining the label. "Never heard of it."

"The good kind. Just drink," Bodhi answered shaking his head. "Burger me, gorgeous," he said to me when he came to the table and sat down.

As I dug a burger out of the bag, Amy said indignantly, "She gets 'gorgeous' and I get 'loserette'?"

Bodhi took the burger, immediately unwrapping it and jamming it into his mouth for a huge bite as he nodded at her. When he swallowed, he said, "You'da greeted me with 'hey, handsome,' maybe you'd get something nicer."

"Duly noted," she replied with a raise of her eyebrows as she took a drink of her beer.

I set both boxes of fries and the other burger in front of him and as he devoured his meal, Amy sat down across from him then getting a wicked gleam in her eyes continued the talk they'd started the last time he'd been over which made me groan and roll my eyes. "So, I still say Batman is way better than Superman." She looked smugly at him.

"You're crazy," he said between bites totally taking her bait. "Superman is practically immortal unless he's exposed to Kryptonite. That's the only thing that can kill him. Batman's human. He's killable."

"Killable?" She snorted. "Is that even a word, Buddha Boy?"

"At least I believe in a higher power, Shabby Douglas," Bodhi shot back making me raise my eyebrows impressed with his name calling ingenuity.

Ignoring his gymnastic barb, Amy retorted, "Oh, my God! Are we going *there* again? Have you ever *seen* a higher power? No! Therefore, it doesn't exist."

"Have you ever seen a thought? Does that mean they don't exist? Jeez, examine every religion and you'll see that each worships a god-like creator."

"Which are made-up beings just like Santa Claus or the Easter Bunny," she shot back.

"Just like you said zombies are made up."

"They are. Have you ever seen a zombie other than in the movies or on TV?"

After a beat Bodhi said, "Well, one thing's for sure," with a sarcastic smile as he wiped his mouth with a napkin.

Amy narrowed her eyes at him. "What's that?"

"If one day we do have a zombie apocalypse, and we know zombies are scavenging for brains, don't worry. You'll be safe."

Just as Amy bowed up, eyes narrowed, ready to spew a shit ton of vitriol right back at him, I shouted, "Guys, stop!"

They stared at each other in silence before Amy muttered, "You'd better be glad I like this beer…"

"And you'd better be glad I like the burgers you bring home," Bodhi mumbled back.

"Can you believe he thinks Superman's better, Scout?" Amy asked me, starting up again. Jeez.

"And can you believe she doesn't believe in a god?" Bodhi threw out.

I held my hands up in surrender. "Don't even try putting me in the middle of your ridiculous arguments."

They looked at me then Amy muttered, "Wimp." They both snickered then she and Bodhi bumped fists, bonding in an unlikely united front against me. Lord.

I shook my head at them, not understanding how their arguing had suddenly cemented their friendship but glad they'd stopped. "Okay, I need help with my movie review. I'm going for comedy this week and was thinking *Anchorman*," I told them.

"I'm in a glass case of emotion," Bodhi quoted.

"I love lamp," Amy added and we were off, throwing every quote we knew out there, which was good because it made them stop their stupid debating, although the quote-fest was now on and could turn ugly between them at any moment if they so chose.

They both helped with the review and after I finished, we ended up watching the movie continuing trying to beat each other by saying the quotes first and arguing over who beat whom. Talk about a competitive group. We also almost finished off the whole case of beer because we'd thrown in having to take a drink if we messed up a quote. I'd messed enough up to make me more than tipsy and feeling pretty good, as was the case with both of them, and when he'd stood up to go to the bathroom and had almost wiped out, I'd informed Bodhi that he was staying. I made up the couch for him by throwing a pillow, sheet and blanket at him, and when I finally flopped into bed, I was at the point of not giving a shit and thought it'd be a fabulous idea to email Gable.

~*~*~*~

From: 9565876 <student.9565876@hallervan.edu>

Subject: You there?

Date: October 4, 12:54 a.m.

To: 9543254 <student.9543254@hallervan.edu>

Yep.

From: 9543254 <student.9543254@hallervan.edu>

Subject: You there?

Date: October 4, 1:00 a.m.

To: 9565876 <student.9565876@hallervan.edu>

Yep? That's it?

From: 9565876 <student.9565876@hallervan.edu>

Subject: You there?

Date: October 4, 1:02 a.m.

To: 9543254 <student.9543254@hallervan.edu>

What else do you wabt?

From: 9543254 <student.9543254@hallervan.edu>

Subject: You there?

Date: October 4, 1:05 a.m.

To: 9565876 <student.9565876@hallervan.edu>

Well, I haven't heard from you in almost two weeks, so I'd like a little more than just Yep. Is there something wrong?

From: 9565876 <student.9565876@hallervan.edu>

Subject: You there?

Date: October 4, 1:07 a.m.

To: 9543254 <student.9543254@hallervan.edu>

Define wtong

From: 9543254 <student.9543254@hallervan.edu>

Subject: You there?

Date: October 4, 1:08 a.m.

To: 9565876 <student.9565876@hallervan.edu>

Has something happened?

From: 9565876 <student.9565876@hallervan.edu>

Subject: You there?

Date: October 4, 1:10 a.m.

To: 9543254 <student.9543254@hallervan.edu>

> Why do you even care?

From: 9543254 <student.9543254@hallervan.edu>

Subject: You there?

Date: October 4, 1:11 a.m.

To: 9565876 <student.9565876@hallervan.edu>

> I guess I'm just worried about you.

Yeah, he'd been so worried about me with his tongue crammed down Alyssa's throat.

From: 9565876 <student.9565876@hallervan.edu>

Subject: You there?

Date: October 4, 1:13 a.m.

To: 9543254 <student.9543254@hallervan.edu>

> I'ts all good

From: 9543254 <student.9543254@hallervan.edu>

Subject: Tipsy?

Date: October 4, 1:14 a.m.

To: 9565876 <student.9565876@hallervan.edu>

Are you drunk?

From: 9565876 <student.9565876@hallervan.edu>

Subject: Tipsy?

Date: October 4, 1:16 a.m.

To: 9543254 <student.9543254@hallervan.edu>

Ding ding ding!

From: 9543254 <student.9543254@hallervan.edu>

Subject: Tipsy?

Date: October 4, 1:17 a.m.

To: 9565876 <student.9565876@hallervan.edu>

Damn. You're unusually hostile. I'm guessing you're a mean drunk. Wish I was there getting trashed with you. I'd put you in a better mood.

From: 9565876 <student.9565876@hallervan.edu>

Subject: Tipsy?

Date: October 4, 1:18 a.m.

To: 9543254 <student.9543254@hallervan.edu>

I'm not a mean drunk just a little mad and how could you put me in a better moood

---

From: 9543254 <student.9543254@hallervan.edu>

Subject: Tipsy?

Date: October 4, 1:19 a.m.

To: 9565876 <student.9565876@hallervan.edu>

What're you mad about? I'd tell you how smart, pretty and sweet you are. You couldn't stay in a bad mood after that. Fuck, you're totally my type, Six.

From: 9565876 <student.9565876@hallervan.edu>

Subject: Tipsy?

Date: October 4, 1:22 a.m.

To: 9543254 <student.9543254@hallervan.edu>

Just am and I don't think I'm your type buut I think you could be mine

I was totally blaming that admission on being drunk.

From: 9543254 <student.9543254@hallervan.edu>

Subject: Tipsy?

Date: October 4, 1:23 a.m.

To: 9565876 <student.9565876@hallervan.edu>

I know I'm you're type. You don't think so? What do you think my type is anyway?

Cocky SOB. I knew what his type was and had to be careful not to inform him that it was Cunt-y Bitch.

From: 9565876 <student.9565876@hallervan.edu>

Subject: Tipsy?

Date: October 4, 1:25 a.m.

What do YOU think your type is

How brilliant was that to put it back on him? I was grinning at my ingenuity when he wrote back.

From: 9565876 <student.9543254@hallervan.edu>

Subject: Tipsy?

Date: October 4, 1:26 a.m.

To: 9565876 <student.9565876@hallervan.edu>

My type would be intelligent, beautiful, funny, confident like you... still curious what you think my type is

Wow. He was anything if not charming.

From: 9565876 <student.9565876@hallervan.edu>

Subject: Tipsy?

Date: October 4, 1:31 a.m.

To: 9543254 <student.9543254@hallervan.edu>

my brother went out with a lot of girls like you, Id have to guess prolly maybe someone whos kinda skanky and easy maybe. I don't want to be mean. I'm sure some are really nice

---

From: 9543254 <student.9543254@hallervan.edu>

Subject: Tipsy?

Date: October 4, 1:33 a.m.

To: 9565876 <student.9565876@hallervan.edu>

I'm laughing right now because you're right. But let me clear something up for you, Six, since you didn't seem to learn this from watching your brother. Guys might go out with girls like that but in the long run they end up with girls like you. You're the kind of girl I'm looking for...I'll PROVE you're my type

I snorted at this because *suuure* I was the kind of girl he wanted since he was an ass to me at every turn. Whatever. I knew better than to trust his sincerity anyway because it was easy to say things when hiding behind the Internet.

From: 9565876 <student.9565876@hallervan.edu>

Subject: Tipsy?

Date: October 4, 1:35 a.m.

To: 9543254 <student.9543254@hallervan.edu>

Wow youre a real charmer arent you

From: 9543254 <student.9543254@hallervan.edu>

Subject: Prince Charming

Date: October 4, 1:37 a.m.

To: 9565876 <student.9565876@hallervan.edu>

I think I can hold my own. Tbh, I'd really like to meet you. I want to see what you look like. It's driving me crazy.

From: 9565876 <student.9565876@hallervan.edu>

Subject: Prince Charming

Date: October 4, 1:40 a.m.

To: 9543254 <student.9543254@hallervan.edu>

No!

From: 9543254 <student.9543254@hallervan.edu>

Subject: Prince Charming

Date: October 4, 1:40 a.m.

To: 9565876 <student.9565876@hallervan.edu>

Come on. This is killing me

From: 9565876 <student.9565876@hallervan.edu>

Subject: Prince Charming

Date: October 4, 1:42 a.m.

To: 9543254 <student.9543254@hallervan.edu>

It's against the rules

From: 9543254 <student.9543254@hallervan.edu>

Subject: Rules are for pussies

Date: October 4, 1:42 a.m.

To: 9565876 <student.9565876@hallervan.edu>

Be a rule breaker with me

No way was that going to happen. Time to go.

From: 9565876 <student.9565876@hallervan.edu>

Subject: Rules are for pussies

Date: October 4, 1:45 a.m.

To: 9543254 <student.9543254@hallervan.edu>

> No... tired now... night

From: 9543254 <student.9543254@hallervan.edu>

Subject: Rules are for pussies

Date: October 4, 1:46 a.m.

To: 9565876 <student.9565876@hallervan.edu>

> Sweet dreams, Six
>
> xx

Pretty sure I passed out staring at my phone, a goofy smile on my face as I took in the kisses he'd sent.

~*~*~*~

The next morning I felt like shit and knew I looked it too as I walked into my psych class. I'd put my hair in a messy bun, had worn no makeup, and topped my jeans with Holden's huge Gonzaga hoodie that I'd stolen. I really wanted to keep my sunglasses on, but I always thought only assholes wore them inside, so I reluctantly slipped them off, immediately squinting at the glow of the fluorescent lights. I climbed the stairs and took my usual seat, put my elbow on the armrest, then rested my forehead in my hand.

I think I drifted off because I startled when I heard a voice in my ear from behind. "Rough night, Priss?"

Gable. Of course.

I'd been doing a really good job of avoiding him this week outside of having to deal with him at the bar, but I guessed my luck just couldn't hold up for long. I shooed him away with my hand and put my head back in my palm, hoping if I ignored him he'd leave me alone.

"What was your poison?"

I let out a deep breath and shook my head. I should've known he was one who couldn't take being ignored. "Seven Seas something," I answered with a groan.

He chuckled, still too close to me. "Nice. 7 Seas Ballz Deep is the shit. Good choice, Priss." He put his hand on my back and rubbed it up and down a couple times which made me stiffen. When he moved his hand up over my hood and started massaging my neck lightly then played with the strands of hair that had fallen out of my bun, I sat straight up pulling away then turning slowly to look at him over my shoulder. "What?" he asked with a slight frown.

"Why're you being nice to me?" I asked, blinking slowly and squinting, the lights in the room still screwing with my head.

He smiled. "I know how it feels, babe. Hangovers are the worst."

I couldn't keep the surprise off my face. *Babe?*

"If you want, after class, I'll take you to my house and make you my hangover cure." He smiled again. Smiled, not grinned, not smirked. *Smiled.*

"Uh… I have another class…"

"Just let me know." He winked then sat back in his chair because Dr. Horner had come in and had started her lecture.

I can't even begin to remember what the lecture was over because all I could do was sit there, head in hand, feeling like shit and wondering what was up with Gable's one-eighty. Was it that he finally figured out I was his pen pal so he was bringing the flirting into real life now? And if he hadn't figured it out, well, he just wasn't trying. I mean, hello, I drunk emailed him last night and now I had a hangover.

But I was curious about where he lived and wanted to see it, but I was also afraid. I mean, who the hell knew what was awaiting me there once he got me alone. Would he keep being nice or revert back to being an asshole which would probably upgrade to *supreme* asshole once he was on his own turf. I finally said, *Fuck it,* because if he really did have a cure for hangovers, I was all in because my head was killing me.

When class was over, I lifted my head gingerly to see Gable crouching on the balls of his feet on the steps to my right watching me, waiting to see what I'd do, his whiskey eyes focused so warmly on mine. I had to close my own eyes for a few seconds after taking him in. God, so handsome. Then curiosity won out. I opened my eyes and gave a small nod at which he smiled then stood and held out his hand. I took it and felt the spark between us again, and gazing up at him, saw that from the baffled look on his face he'd felt it too. So weird.

What was even weirder was the fact that he was being so sweet to me, which of course just made me fall a little bit more for him.

And wasn't that just wonderful.

~*~*~*~

Ever been hated by hundreds of women at once? That's what it was like when Gable and I walked outside the psychology building, him still holding my hand as he led me to his car. I would've pulled my hand from his, but I was walking with my eyes half closed trying to keep as much sun out as possible because I'd forgotten to put on my sunglasses, my head hurt too much for me to make any sudden movements, and also I think I must've still been a little drunk.

Yeah, we'll just go with all that, shall we?

But it seemed that every woman we passed was glaring at me like she hated my guts.

"So, I get the feeling that I'm not the most popular person on campus right now," I mumbled. He glanced down at me waiting for me to explain. "Look at them. They're all giving me the evil eye." I nodded at one particularly vengeful looking vamp.

He looked around as we walked then chuckled.

"So how many of them have you gone out with?" I asked.

He knocked his arm into my shoulder playfully. "Why? Jealous?"

"God, not that again." I frowned.

He snorted.

"Seriously, how many?" I persisted. I had to admit it was kind of fascinating watching these women's faces when they saw that Gable and I held hands, the astonishment, the acrimony and envy that they shot in my direction at thinking he was with me.

"A few."

"Hm."

I knew that should've made me more than wary about him and that I shouldn't let my mind go where it was currently going, but I was honestly thrilled at just holding hands with him and let myself imagine for a few minutes that we really were together and I was the envy of every woman on campus.

As I studied him out of the corner of my eye watching him walking so confidently by my side with not a care in the world, it just made me sigh, checking out how hot he was in his olive green military jacket over a maroon Hallervan hoodie, faded jeans and the brown boots I'd seen him wearing before. He wasn't wearing his glasses, but that just made his eyes even more striking. He had about two days' worth of scruff covering his square jaw and all I could do was shake my head at how damned good looking he was.

As we walked, I kicked around the theory of how people seemed to take more shit from good looking people and how, if I wasn't so attracted to him, I'd already have written Gable off some time ago because of his rudeness. I decided this was something I needed to ask Dr. Horner about because it left me feeling a little shallow.

We made it to the parking lot where there were puddles of water everywhere, and, God help me, I knew I was in so much trouble (and that my aforementioned theory was shot to hell) when Gable peered down at me with his lazy grin then suddenly scooped me up in his arms bridal style making me yelp as I laced my arms around his neck and he carried me to his car. "Can't have you getting your feet wet," he mumbled with a smile as he himself walked through the small pools of water the recent rain had left.

Oh, my God. Most romantic thing anyone had ever done for me. My heart definitely took a hit with that one.

When we got to his car, he set me on my feet, and adding to the giddiness I was still feeling from his carrying me, I saw that he drove absolutely what I'd pictured he'd drive—a cherry red 1970 Chevelle. Badass muscle car. Of course.

"My oldest brother used to have the same car but his was black," I said quietly, still reeling from how sweet he was being to me.

"He has good taste," he said with a grin as he opened the passenger door for me. I got in and he leaned across me, grabbing the seatbelt and pulling it across my lap. "It's tricky," he explained as he messed with it then turned toward me and his face was *right there*, his lips not an inch from mine. We stared at each other for a moment and when my eyes slid down to his mouth, I saw the sides of it tip up. My eyes jumped back up to see his dancing with amusement as a smile formed on his beautiful face. Shit. I turned away quickly feeling the heat rising in my cheeks as he finished buckling me in then closed my door, going around to get in the driver's side.

"Stop," I muttered to myself before he got in, reminding myself I'd only end up getting hurt if I wasn't careful.

Breathing in the smell of the leather seats, I was suddenly blasted with a bit of nostalgia for home and when he got in and fired up the Chevelle, tears suddenly stung the backs of my eyes because it reminded me so much of Heath and made me miss him and Holden and Dad terribly.

"You okay?" Gable asked, glancing over at me, his brow furrowed.

A tear escaped and I brushed it from my cheek. "Yeah, I'm fine. Sorry. Your car just reminds me of home."

He reached over and squeezed my hand, smiling at me, and, dear God, if he didn't stop being so nice, I was going to fall to pieces right there and have a big boohoo-fest. But he did stop when he moved his hand to the gearshift and put it in reverse, backing up, then threw it into first and we took off.

"Where *is* home, Scout?" he asked and my head swung to him as I gaped at him in surprise. "What?" he asked.

"I didn't know you knew my name," I said stupidly immediately wincing because, of course, he knew my name. We worked together. We had class together. Good gosh.

He chuckled. "Yeah, that stuff has a way of getting out at O'Leary's. Oh, wait, did I blow your cover or something?" He grinned over at me and if I was any lesser a woman, I'd have completely melted right there in my seat. But I was a strong, hardworking farm girl, so I only had a mild stroke taking in his handsome face and then just a teeny amount of arrhythmia flared up when he winked at me.

Holy damn.

"Yeah, that was dumb," I mumbled, turning to glance out my window through half-closed eyes, the sun still too bright for my hungover self.

"So?"

I turned back to him in question.

"Where're you from?" he repeated with a chuckle.

Oh. Duh. "Stone Springs."

He looked over at me again and gave me his half grin throwing in a raised eyebrow trying to slay me even more, I supposed. "Stone Springs, you say... so, would that be in Alaska? Florida? Outer Mongolia?"

I laughed in spite of feeling like an idiot. "Idaho."

"Ah," he muttered. "So what's there to do in Stone Springs?"

I shrugged. "Not a whole lot. We own a farm, we have a pond to swim in, so there's that."

"No movie theater? Bowling? Quarterly purges?"

Well, wasn't Gable a funny guy. "Smartass. We have a little theater but it only shows two movies at a time every two months, so there's not a huge variety. If we want to bowl, we have to go to Idaho Falls. And purges are only bi-annually, so we have to make them count."

He laughed. "Who's the smartass now?" We rode in silence for a while before he asked, "So, you've got a brother?"

"Two, actually. Both older." I knew I had to be careful here because I'd told him quite a bit about my family in our emails and if he hadn't already figured things out, I didn't want to give myself away. God, this whole pen pal thing had taken on an evil life of its own.

"Yeah? What are *their* names? Tonto and Lone Ranger?" I watched as he chuckled, and, boy, did he look good chuckling. The indentions around the sides of his mouth were even attractive. Dang.

"Good one. Never heard that before." I rolled my eyes. "Heath and Holden. They're seven and four years older than I am."

"Sisters?" he asked, glancing over at me.

"No."

"You're the baby, huh?" He winked at me again and I had to concentrate on keeping my mouth from hanging open.

"Yeah. So, what about you? Brothers? Sisters?"

"Three brothers. Zeke's a senior, plays football. Ryker's a sophomore wrestler and Loch's a freshman." He gave me a quick glance.

"Wow. Your poor mom."

He laughed. "Yeah. Always had at least two in diapers for years. Believe me, she lets us know all the time what little hellions we were."

"What about your dad?"

"What about him?" He smiled as he kept his eyes on the road.

"What does he do?" I knew he was a mechanic, but it was fascinating hearing it all from him for some reason.

"He's a mechanic. Part owner of a garage with my uncle. That's where we picked up Lucille."

I frowned. "Lucille?"

"Lucille," he said, patting his steering wheel. "She's my girl. Had her since I was a sophomore in high school."

I nodded. I totally got the whole naming your car thing. My Honda was named Adam Morrison for the star basketball forward from Gonzaga. As I sat thinking how Morrison's pro career hadn't quite worked out, I noticed that we'd entered a neighborhood and Gable had now turned onto a street then parked in front of a cute cottage-style house. We were behind a black pickup, which seemed to be the same one he'd driven the day he'd stopped to help me with my tire. There was also a blue pickup in the driveway along with what appeared to be a sixty-something orange Mustang.

"Home sweet home," he said looking over at me.

"Gable lives in a house with five gables," I replied peering out my window.

"How do you know that?" He put his right arm across the back of my seat and playfully tugged a piece of my hair that'd gotten free.

I shivered when he rested his hand on my shoulder, then pulling myself out of my *I Can't Help Going Gaga Over Gable* zone, shrugged. "Guess I must've heard my dad talking about them at some point."

He nodded with his lips pooched out. "Impressive. I've been leaning toward going into architecture, actually taking a couple classes right now, so I'm seriously impressed that you knew that." He got out of the car and I watched him walk around moving so smoothly and I got so caught up in ogling him that I jumped when he opened my door. Once again he leaned in to unbuckle me and his beautiful face was right there. Those perfect lips were *right there*. All I had to do was lean in, like, two centimeters and we'd be kissing. God. While I was staring at his mouth, I realized he'd gotten my seatbelt undone and was facing me at close range now. My eyes moved slowly to his and I found I couldn't breathe. "Your eyes are beautiful, Scout," he whispered.

And then he was gone, standing up outside the car and holding his hand out to help me out.

Holy crap.

I pulled in a deep breath through my nose and reached out to take his hand as I got out of the car on wobbly legs. Jeez.

"Zeke, Ryker and I live here," he explained with a grin, still holding my hand as we went up the walk. "Loch still lives at home with Mom and Dad, but he hangs out here a lot."

Oh, great. A house where three grown men lived. I braced myself for a blast of yucky man-smell and what would surely be a mess when we got to the door, but once inside, it surprisingly smelled like someone had made cookies and the whole place was rather neat. I looked up at him in what I know was surprise.

"Mom comes by on the weekends and puts us to work cleaning," he explained, knowing exactly what my look was for.

Right off the bat I saw that the living room housed a huge TV that was currently airing a football game and there was a sofa and two recliners facing it, each of which was currently occupied by huge bodies that were watching the game.

"What's up?" a guy in one of the recliners, straining his head back, asked, and, good God, he appeared to be an older, slightly larger version of Gable, meaning he too was hot. He wore jeans, a black Bulldogs sweatshirt and running shoes, his long legs stretched out, feet crossed at the ankle on the leg rest.

"Hangover," Gable replied, still holding my hand and nodding toward me, which made my cheeks flush in embarrassment. "That's my older brother Zeke." I waved lamely at him as he gave me a chin raise. "That's Ryker," he said, nodding to the muscular, silent guy, another Gable clone, lying on his back on the couch wearing a gray sweat suit and socks. He nodded at me as I did the lame wave again. Ugh. "And that's Loch." He nodded at the other recliner where a younger Gable look-alike sat, who was dressed similarly to Gable, and who was now smiling at me. "This is Scout Patterson," Gable told them all.

"Hi," I mumbled, waving again like a dork.

"I think you're in my biology class," the youngest one, Loch, said, narrowing his eyes at me looking just as Gable had the first day of psych when he was trying to place where he'd seen me.

I raised my eyebrows at him. "Yeah?"

"Yeah. You sit in the second row, third seat, middle section, right?"

"Uh…"

"Loch's like an idiot savant, noticing stupid shit like that," Gable informed me with a chuckle.

"Fuck off," Loch retorted good naturedly, flipping Gable the bird.

Gable let my hand go and walked to where Loch was sitting. "Fuck off? *Fuck off?*" he asked. "You kiss your mother with that mouth?" he added then grabbed his little brother in a headlock and proceeded to scrub his fisted knuckles over his head.

"Dude! The hair!" Loch cried, wrestling himself away from Gable, then frowning went to the mirror that hung by the door to do damage control on his hair as Gable laughed at him and called him a pussy which made him frown even more.

"You get that belt Dad told you to pick up?" the guy lying on the couch asked. Ryker, that was his name.

"Yeah. It's in the car. We can work on the Mustang tonight if you want," Gable told him.

"Gotta meet."

Ah, Ryker was the wrestler.

"I'll fix it myself then," Gable said shrugging his shoulders. "Gotta work at six, though." He turned back to me and smiled, taking my hand once again and leading me into the kitchen. At the bar, he pulled a stool out for me. "Have a seat and I'll fix you up."

The throb in my head had downgraded to a dull thump and I watched as he opened a cabinet under the counter and pulled out a blender then moved to the fridge to get some things out. While he did this, I looked around the place to see that the beige wall in the living room that I could see had a couple pictures of what I assumed was Seattle at night and a few framed photo collages of the brothers. Looking back at the kitchen I saw a big, round clock hanging over the rectangular table and some kind of hotrod pinup calendar was magneted to the freezer door of the refrigerator with a bikini-clad woman on it lying across the hood of a silver Camaro. The walls in the kitchen were robin's egg blue and the cabinets were a light oak. I could tell it was a nice house and had been well taken care of.

"Okay, might wanna cover your ears," Gable said.

I looked at him and he nodded at the blender. Oh. I put my hands over ears right before he pressed a button on it then grinned at me before turning to watch whatever he'd put in it mixing around. A moment later he glanced back at me and nodded. I took my hands away from my ears and smiled in gratitude at him. He pulled a glass out of a cabinet near the sink then took the jar out of the base of the blender and poured a semi-thick, reddish concoction into the glass.

Walking over to me, he placed the glass on the bar in front of me. "Works every time."

I eyed the glass then gave him a semi-skeptical look.

"Seriously. Drink up," he said, pushing the glass closer to me.

I hesitated for a second, now questioning if this really was a good idea as my stomach churned. He pushed it even closer, so I picked it up and took a sniff of it first then took a tentative sip. When I didn't puke immediately, I went ahead and took a careful drink. Hm. Not bad.

"Gatorade, vanilla ice cream and two bananas," he said proudly.

That made sense. The drink was loaded with potassium and electrolytes, well, except for the ice cream, and since it didn't sound or taste too bad, I drank the rest of it down as he cleaned up. "Thank you," I said when I finished and noticed that I was already feeling a little better, probably because I hadn't eaten anything that morning and now had something in my belly. "Your recipe?"

"An old family one," he said with a chuckle as he put the blender jar in the fridge and the base away back under the cabinet. "Better?"

I nodded. "Yeah, I think so." I smiled.

"Good." He walked over and leaned down on his forearms on the bar looking at me like a doctor assessing a patient. "Need more?"

"No, I think this'll do it. Thanks." And as my head started clearing, I realized how strange this whole thing was. Gable had brought me to his house, he'd introduced me to his brothers and he'd made me a hangover cure and he hadn't even been rude to me. Crazy.

Speaking of rude, I remembered something. "Hey, what happened to your friend who was in psych the first day?" I asked.

"Justin? Dropped out."

He now glanced at the clock above the table. "Well, I've got a class at ten, so I need to get back."

"Yeah, me too. French. It's going to kick my ass." I chuckled.

I watched as he turned his head slightly to the side as he studied me, eyes narrowing. Oh, shit. I'd talked about French in my emails. I'd said almost the same exact thing in my email. Ack! I held my breath and kept my face as innocent as I could until he finally replied, still looking at me pensively, "Calculus will probably do that to mine. Ready?"

Okay. I knew this entire thing was stupid. I mean, why didn't I just tell him we were writing to each other instead of acting like it was a case of national security? But I think maybe the reason I didn't tell him was that it'd gone on for so long now and he'd been so nice in his emails that I think I just wanted that part of him to myself, and that the intrigue he felt toward his unknown pen pal was flattering and I sort of loved the attention from him even though it really wasn't me he was writing to. Yeah, I know. Confusing. And dumb.

So instead of confessing, I nodded and took the hand that he offered and stepped down from the barstool immediately noticing that my headache was gone. "You're a miracle worker." I playfully knocked my shoulder into his arm.

He was still looking at me speculatively, but he didn't say anything as he walked us back through the living room. "We're out," he told his brothers.

"It was nice meeting you all," I said shyly and heard their mumbled replies as they nodded cursorily at me before their attention went back to the TV which I could've taken as being rude, but then I realized that they were probably used to Gable bringing multiple girls home, so it wasn't like I was anything special. To them, they probably thought I was just another chick he was going to bang. And wasn't that humbling.

He walked me out to the car, opened my door for me, leaned in and put my seatbelt on but didn't say a word or even give me a look. After closing my door, he went around, got in and drove me back to campus in complete silence. When we got back on campus, he drove into the same parking lot since the liberal arts building was near Old North where our psych class was, but he pulled up to the curb so I wouldn't have to step in any of the puddles. "My class is across campus," he said, as he reached over to undo my seatbelt, and I found I was disappointed that he'd passed on coming around to lean over me to do it. When I got out, I bent down to look at him, seeing that he was still watching me closely.

"Thanks again," I muttered and at his troubled nod, I closed the door then watched him drive away.

Yep. Pretty sure he'd figured it out.

Week Seven

From: 9565876 <student.9565876@hallervan.edu>

Subject: Hi =)

Date: October 7, 8:16 a.m.

To: 9543254 <student.9543254@hallervan.edu>

> Four,
>
> Just wanted to tell you to have a great week!
>
> See ya!
>
> Six
>
> xo

~*~*~*~

Gable didn't write back that week. He didn't talk to me in class. He didn't do anything. I saw him all three days and he acted as if I didn't exist. I worked two nights and he filled my orders with no smartass comebacks or reckless flirting. Nothing.

And this really got to me.

"He's got to know I'm his pen pal. I mean, he's stopped talking to me both in real life and through email," I said to Bodhi Friday at lunch in the student center.

He finished his first grilled cheese in two bites and picked up his second one. "Sounds like it."

"I mean, why else would he be ignoring me?"

"Maybe he has issues with girls."

I huffed out a humorless laugh. "I don't think that's his problem."

"I mean, yeah, he's pretty hot and the girls flock to him, but what I'm saying is maybe his issues are that he's afraid of getting *close* to girls. Perhaps he felt he was getting too close to you." He shrugged. "Could've had a bad breakup or something," he said as an afterthought.

I tapped my pencil against my lips. "You're probably right. We were emailing about exes a while back and he didn't want to talk about his. That's gotta be it." I now chewed on the eraser of my pencil. Then it hit me. "So you're saying the reason he's avoiding me is because he started getting close to me and it scared him off?"

Bodhi held a finger up while chewing on a mouthful of fries. When he swallowed he grabbed his bottle of water and took a big drink. "You're a sharp one, Scout."

I frowned at his sarcasm. "Are you sure? Why would he suddenly become afraid that we were getting too close?" I looked off in the distance as I mulled that over before looking back at him. "Unless he knows I'm his pen pal. So it's not that we were getting too close in real life, it's just that if he knows we're writing to each other too, that made him back off. God, this is so confusing." I shook my head. "I should've just told him."

"It *is* confusing." He shoved more fries in his mouth. "And, yeah, maybe you should've told him, but look, if I had to guess, from what you told me, I'd say he's definitely suspicious about it which may have scared him away. But it still sounds as if he's interested since he said you're his type." He thought about this for a few seconds as he took a drink. "But I guess that was to pen pal you." He frowned. "But I still think he likes real life you but he's staying away since he suspects you're also his pen pal."

Wow. This was so totally confusing.

"And he's pissed because he opened up to me through email?" I said.

"I don't know. It's easier to hide behind the Internet and talk to someone because you can always disappear at any time." He took a big bite of his brownie then with his mouth still full said, "Bottom line is, he's shared some personal things with you in his emails and if he thinks you're his pen pal that might be a little threatening to him because he doesn't want to get close to real life you."

I took a deep breath and let it out in a big sigh. "This is ridiculous. I hate this assignment." I reached over and tore a piece of his brownie off which got me a hand slap. After throwing the piece in my mouth I said somewhat deflated, "I told him in my email that he was my type too." I shook my head at my stupidity.

Bodhi gave a half shrug. "Nothing wrong with that. You're attracted to him. I get it. The heart wants what the heart wants."

And that made me feel not so stupid. "God, I love you." I leaned over and kissed his cheek. "You always make me feel better about being an idiot."

He grinned as he downed the rest of his brownie.

"But do you think what I've done is deceitful? Knowing who he is and all? Would you be mad?" I asked.

"You figured it out to begin with, right? Your friend at the paper just validated your suspicions. Nah, I wouldn't be mad, I don't think. I think I'd actually use it to my advantage and fuck with you some."

"You think he's gonna fuck with me?" I was trying not to think about him fucking with me in any way because it was very distracting when my phone dinged that I had an email. I pulled it out of my jacket pocket and almost fell out of my chair. "It's him!" I whispered, peering up at Bodhi, kind of scared shitless for some reason.

"What'd he say?"

"He said again that he wants to meet. But that's against the rules! What do I do?"

Bodhi laughed. "Answer him, dork. Why're you freaking out?"

"We can't meet! If he knows it's me and he knows that I knew it was him, he'll know I knew and I know he *will* be mad and he'll never talk to me again. But that might be a good thing because nothing's ever going to happen with us anyway because in real life I don't think he's really interested in me." My eyes started filling with tears as I refuted everything Bodhi'd just said. "Oh, God." I grabbed a napkin and dabbed at my eyes. How ridiculous was I? "I guess I didn't think he'd talk to me again. What's wrong with me?"

Bodhi shook his head then reached over and took my phone. "You're PMSing."

My head shot up and I scowled at him. "What? How'd you know?"

"Amy is too. She was particularly mean last night, so I thought that must be it. You two are probably synced now since you live together."

I blinked at him. Then I blinked again. "Uh. Kinda creepy, Bode. And how the hell do you know this stuff?"

He gave me a "get real" look. "I lived with my sister and mom. Believe me, Dad and I always made ourselves scarce when they were both hormonal." He started typing something into my phone.

"Bodhi! What are you writing?" I shrieked trying to grab my phone from him.

He held it away from me as he typed then finally handed it back while I had a mini panic attack. "Gotta get to class. I'll see you this weekend sometime, 'kay?"

I nodded absentmindedly, poking around on my phone trying to see what he'd written, barely noticing it when he bent and kissed my forehead before he left.

From: 9565876 <student.9565876@hallervan.edu>

Subject: Rendezvous

Date: October 11, 12:33 p.m.

To: 9543254 <student.9543254@hallervan.edu>

We have to follow the rules. If we didn't have rules, the world would be a messy place

Oh, good one, Bodhi. I looked up to see him dumping the contents of his tray into a trashcan near the door, and when he twisted his head to look back at me, I gave him a big smile and a thumbs up which made him grin and shake his head before he turned and left the student center.

Then my phone dinged again.

From: 9543254 <student.9543254@hallervan.edu>

Subject: Again with the rules

Date: October 11, 12:36 p.m.

To: 9565876 <student.9565876@hallervan.edu>

Rules were meant to be broken

I didn't realize how much I'd missed talking to Gable and I closed my eyes in relief that the stalemate had ended. And, damn it, I wasn't going to be a coward any longer. If he was avoiding me because he felt he was getting too close then he'd just have to get over it. I was interested in him, as in, I really liked him, and he'd said pen pal me was his type, even if he didn't really mean it about real life me, but maybe if I kept things light, he'd get past the not wanting to get closer part and move forward with this which could continue over to our real lives.

Ugh. I'll take a shot of baffling with a side of befuddlement, please.

I rolled my eyes at how ridiculous I'd let things get as I typed a message back.

From: 9565876 <student.9565876@hallervan.edu>

Subject: Cliché

Date: October 11, 12:38 p.m.

To: 9543254 <student.9543254@hallervan.edu>

Said every cliché user ever

From: 9543254 <student.9543254@hallervan.edu>

Subject: Cliché

Date: October 11, 12:41 p.m.

To: 9565876 <student.9565876@hallervan.edu>

That's me, a walking cliché

From: 9565876 <student.9565876@hallervan.edu>

Subject: Doubtful

Date: October 11, 12:43 p.m.

To: 9543254 <student.9543254@hallervan.edu>

I highly doubt that. So where've you been?

From: 9543254 <student.9543254@hallervan.edu>

Subject: Doubtful

Date: October 11, 12:43 p.m.

To: 9565876 <student.9565876@hallervan.edu>

Had some shit to sort out

From: 9565876 <student.9565876@hallervan.edu>

Subject: Doubtful

Date: October 11, 12:44 p.m.

To: 9543254 <student.9543254@hallervan.edu>

Yeah? Care to share?

From: 9543254 <student.9543254@hallervan.edu>

Subject: Doubtful

Date: October 11, 12:44 p.m.

To: 9565876 <student.9565876@hallervan.edu>

Just some personal stuff

From: 9565876 <student.9565876@hallervan.edu>

Subject: Doubtful

Date: October 11, 12:44 p.m.

To: 9543254 <student.9543254@hallervan.edu>

    Oh, okay

From: 9543254 <student.9543254@hallervan.edu>

Subject: Curious

Date: October 11, 12:45 p.m.

To: 9565876 <student.9565876@hallervan.edu>

    So what're you doing?

From: 9565876 <student.9565876@hallervan.edu>

Subject: Curious

Date: October 11, 12:45 p.m.

To: 9543254 <student.9543254@hallervan.edu>

    Eating lunch in the student center

From: 9543254 <student.9543254@hallervan.edu>

Subject: Still curious

Date: October 11, 12:45 p.m.

To: 9565876 <student.9565876@hallervan.edu>

    What're you having?

From: 9565876 <student.9565876@hallervan.edu>

Subject: Still curious

Date: October 11, 12:45 p.m.

To: 9543254 <student.9543254@hallervan.edu>

Burrito surprise o_O

From: 9543254 <student.9543254@hallervan.edu>

Subject: Still curious

Date: October 11, 12:46 p.m.

To: 9565876 <student.9565876@hallervan.edu>

My favorite ;)

From: 9565876 <student.9565876@hallervan.edu>

Subject: Um

Date: October 11, 12:46 p.m.

To: 9543254 <student.9543254@hallervan.edu>

Uh. You do know what the surprise is, right?

From: 9543254 <student.9543254@hallervan.edu>

Subject: Um

Date: October 11, 12:46 p.m.

To: 9565876 <student.9565876@hallervan.edu>

Hell yeah, I do. They put a hotdog in the middle of the burrito. That shit's fucking awesome

---

From: 9565876 <student.9565876@hallervan.edu>

Subject: Gross

Date: October 11, 12:47 p.m.

To: 9543254 <student.9543254@hallervan.edu>

OMG It's disgusting. My friend tried to warn me, but I was curious. You on campus?

From: 9543254 <student.9543254@hallervan.edu>

Subject: Delectable shit

Date: October 11, 12:47 p.m.

To: 9565876 <student.9565876@hallervan.edu>

Your taste buds must be on the blink 'cause that shit's the shit. Yep.

From: 9565876 <student.9565876@hallervan.edu>

Subject: Delusional

Date: October 11, 12:47 p.m.

To: 9543254 <student.9543254@hallervan.edu>

Tell you what. I'll leave my tray on the table. There are two burritos untouched. Well, the first one's a little mutilated because I kinda hacked it open trying to find what the surprise was. Anyway, I'm leaving, so it's all yours. They'll be on one of the tables closest to the windows

---

From: 9543254 <student.9543254@hallervan.edu>

Subject: Lucid as hell

Date: October 11, 12:48 p.m.

To: 9565876 <student.9565876@hallervan.edu>

Sweet. I'll be there in 5

Shit! I hoped he was kidding.

From: 9543254 <student.9543254@hallervan.edu>

Subject: Lucid as hell

Date: October 11, 12:48 p.m.

To: 9565876 <student.9565876@hallervan.edu>

Kidding. Headed home for lunch with my bros

Thank God!

From: 9543254 <student.9543254@hallervan.edu>

Subject: Lucid as hell

Date: October 11, 12:48 p.m.

To: 9565876 <student.9565876@hallervan.edu>

But I AM tempted to go to the SC to see who you are… ;)

From: 9565876 <student.9565876@hallervan.edu>

Subject: Sea of women

Date: October 11, 12:49 p.m.

To: 9543254 <student.9543254@hallervan.edu>

Jsyk there are tons of girls here enjoying this fine entrée. It'd be kinda tough to know which one's me

---

From: 9543254 <student.9543254@hallervan.edu>

Subject: Six radar

Date: October 11, 12:50 p.m.

To: 9565876 <student.9565876@hallervan.edu>

Oh, I think I could pick you out

From: 9565876 <student.9565876@hallervan.edu>

Subject: Six radar

Date: October 11, 12:50 p.m.

To: 9543254 <student.9543254@hallervan.edu>

How?!

From: 9543254 <student.9543254@hallervan.edu>

Subject: Obvious

Date: October 11, 12:51 p.m.

To: 9565876 <student.9565876@hallervan.edu>

You'd be the one emailing with the goofy grin on your face and guarding a full tray of deliciousness

---

From: 9565876 <student.9565876@hallervan.edu>

Subject: I'd rather eat my shoe

Date: October 11, 12:51 p.m.

To: 9543254 <student.9543254@hallervan.edu>

Ha deliciousness my ass

From: 9543254 <student.9543254@hallervan.edu>

Subject: Beautiful backside

Date: October 11, 12:51 p.m.

To: 9565876 <student.9565876@hallervan.edu>

I'll just bet your ass is delicious

From: 9565876 <student.9565876@hallervan.edu>

Subject: Beautiful backside

Date: October 11, 12:53 p.m.

To: 9543254 <student.9543254@hallervan.edu>

From: 9543254 <student.9543254@hallervan.edu>

Subject: Hot

Date: October 11, 12:53 p.m.

To: 9565876 <student.9565876@hallervan.edu>

C'mon, Six. I know you've gotta have a rockin' body

From: 9565876 <student.9565876@hallervan.edu>

Subject: Hot

Date: October 11, 12:53 p.m.

To: 9543254 <student.9543254@hallervan.edu>

How am I supposed to answer that?

From: 9543254 <student.9543254@hallervan.edu>

Subject: Hot

Date: October 11, 12:53 p.m.

To: 9565876 <student.9565876@hallervan.edu>

> By telling me what you're wearing

I surveyed the student center, a bit paranoid. What if he was in here watching me because he'd figured it out? After scouring the place and not seeing him, I decided to give him a bit of his own flirty medicine.

From: 9565876 <student.9565876@hallervan.edu>

Subject: You asked

Date: October 11, 12:55 p.m.

To: 9543254 <student.9543254@hallervan.edu>

> A black bustier, thong and garter belt with black stockings under a black pencil skirt, white button down shirt tucked in and my black stilettos

---

From: 9543254 <student.9543254@hallervan.edu>

Subject: Fuck... me

Date: October 11, 12:55 p.m.

To: 9565876 <student.9565876@hallervan.edu>

> Fuck... me

Uh, yes, please.

From: 9565876 <student.9565876@hallervan.edu>

Subject: Too much?

Date: October 11, 12:55 p.m.

To: 9543254 <student.9543254@hallervan.edu>

You like?

From: 9543254 <student.9543254@hallervan.edu>

Subject: Perfect

Date: October 11, 12:56 p.m.

To: 9565876 <student.9565876@hallervan.edu>

Hell yeah. Tell me you're not really wearing that... if you are, I'm turning around and coming back to find you in the SC

From: 9565876 <student.9565876@hallervan.edu>

Subject: Kidding

Date: October 11, 12:56 p.m.

To: 9543254 <student.9543254@hallervan.edu>

lol Just messing with you

From: 9543254 <student.9543254@hallervan.edu>

Subject: Damn

Date: October 11, 12:56 p.m.

To: 9565876 <student.9565876@hallervan.edu>

That was one helluva visual

From: 9565876 <student.9565876@hallervan.edu>

Subject: Wait

Date: October 11, 12:56 p.m.

To: 9543254 <student.9543254@hallervan.edu>

Wait. You're not emailing and driving are you???

From: 9543254 <student.9543254@hallervan.edu>

Subject: Guilty

Date: October 11, 12:57 p.m.

To: 9565876 <student.9565876@hallervan.edu>

...

From: 9565876 <student.9565876@hallervan.edu>

Subject: Law breaker

Date: October 11, 12:45 p.m.

To: 9543254 <student.9543254@hallervan.edu>

STOP right NOW!

From: 9543254 <student.9543254@hallervan.edu>

Subject: Dominatrix

Date: October 11, 12:57 p.m.

To: 9565876 <student.9565876@hallervan.edu>

I love it when you're bossy. That shit's hot…

From: 9565876 <student.9565876@hallervan.edu>

Subject: Not funny

Date: October 11, 12:57 p.m.

To: 9543254 <student.9543254@hallervan.edu>

I'm not answering you back until I know you're not driving. It's illegal to be on your phone anyway. You'll get pulled over

---

From: 9543254 <student.9543254@hallervan.edu>

Subject: I got this

Date: October 11, 12:58 p.m.

To: 9565876 <student.9565876@hallervan.edu>

Not me. I'm kind of a cool character, Six. Haven't you figured that out yet?

I didn't answer and I wouldn't until I knew he wasn't driving. And, yes, I knew he was a cool character. He'd proven it time and again.

~*~*~*~

Gable was back to his old self at work that night. And I kind of liked that he was. It was better than being ignored by him.

Damn. I was sick in the head.

"We're mortal enemies, Priss," he said with a sly smile when I set my tray on the bar.

I frowned not knowing what he was talking about. He nodded at our jerseys.

"You're wearing the Giants. I'm wearing the Patriots. Just won't work."

"Well, darn, since we were *such* great friends before this, that just breaks my heart," I replied with a roll of my eyes. "Maybe I should change into a different jersey so we'll be friends again." If he could be a cool character, I could as well, so I'd just continue being my smartassed self when it came to him.

"Technically, everyone's a rival of the Patriots so it wouldn't matter what you changed into." He chuckled.

I had no idea about pro football so I shook my head and watched as he filled my order. I might've watched his butt a little too, but I couldn't help myself.

After setting the beers on my tray, he leaned over the counter and said low, "Your ass looks particularly delicious tonight, Priss."

My eyes got huge as I stared at him. He'd said pretty much the same in his email. He had to know! He gave me an impish grin then turned away, going to wait on a customer leaving me standing there with my mouth hanging open.

A little unsettled, I picked up my tray and walked away to deliver the drinks to my customers. Okay, so the jig was up. No big deal. We were both now culpable for keeping it secret. But because I was as stubborn as I was, I was going to leave it to him to 'fess up first.

Oh, and maybe because I was a huge coward.

~*~*~*~

I took a break at ten going out back to get some air when the door opened a few minutes later. Gable.

"You stalking me?" I asked giving him a sneer from where I stood leaning against the wall and drinking a bottle of water.

"Maybe," he answered, the half grin making an appearance as he walked toward me, his beautiful brown eyes on mine.

"Wh-what are you doing?" I stammered when he stopped right in front of me. I set my water bottle on a milk crate next to me and wondered what he was up to as I looked up at him, half panicking.

He looked down at me, his eyes dancing with mirth at seeing how uncomfortable I'd grown. "You feel it as much as I do, Priss. The sexual tension between us could be cut with a fucking knife." His lips curled up as he watched the alarm flash across my face.

Oh, my God. Was he playing with me? If so, I'd kill him.

He pressed me back against the wall and the next thing I knew his hands came up to hold my face. "Why don't we just give in?" Before I knew what was happening his mouth was on mine.

Holy shit!

And, wow, his lips were as soft as I knew they'd be. And he tasted wonderful, all minty and fresh. And his body. Dear baby Jesus. It was as hard as I thought it'd be… and he was hard everywhere. Wow. When he thrust his tongue inside my mouth to tangle with mine, I found myself gripping his shoulders, pulling him closer as I emitted a huge whore moan. It'd been a while since I'd been kissed, and right now I was kissing Gable Powers and just couldn't help myself.

His hands moved down my neck and over my shoulders then slid around to my back then lower where he grabbed my butt pulling me flush against him as our smoking hot kiss continued. Oh, God, I was so wet for him, feeling him so hard against my bare stomach and I knew I was losing myself in him when my leg came up and curled around the back of his as I ground myself against his thigh wanting more. More. *More!* Oh, my God, I'd never wanted anyone as much as I wanted him.

His lips moved over my jaw to a spot below my ear that he sucked lightly, making me shiver in his arms. One of his hands slid around to my belly, the backs of his fingers smoothing sensually across my exposed skin then he turned his hand to where his palm was flat against me and I felt it glide down where the tips of his fingers slipped just inside my jeans. Oh, God, yes!

"Mmm, you taste good," he muttered against my neck and I froze.

Wait. What?

And that became the moment of my getting a fucking clue.

My hands suddenly moved from his shoulders to his chest and I shoved him away from me hard, and glory be to all things holy, he actually went back on a foot.

"Are you kidding me!" I spat.

He jerked his head back in surprise, narrowing his eyes at me.

"I'm not Alyssa!"

"Didn't say you were," he answered, his brow creased as if he had no clue what I was talking about.

"I'm not one of your easy lays either!" I turned my head away, pissed that I'd gotten so carried away with that damned kiss.

He put a hand against the wall to the side of my head and gripped my chin with the fingers of his other turning my head back, making me look at him. "Didn't say that either."

I jerked my chin out of his hand and ducked under his arm, spinning to face him, hands on my hips. "You're unbelievable! The night you and Alyssa were out here, you said the same thing to her!"

I saw the shock on his face for a second before it disappeared but he just kept watching me as I glared at him, my lips still tingling from that fabulous freakin' kiss. Damn him.

"I know you're not like them, Priss," he replied, taking a step toward me.

I took a step back, holding my palm up in warning for him to stay back. "Yeah? Well, since that seems to be what you're looking for, you need to stay the fuck away from me," I hissed then turned and went back inside quickly making my way to the bathroom where I looked at myself in the mirror, wiping away the tears that'd made their way down my cheeks. How could I have been so stupid to think I was something special to him? God!

The rest of the night was just fabulous as I continued having to get orders filled by him, ignoring him as he tried at first apologizing then getting angrier by the minute when he acted as if nothing had happened between us and he was back in flirty asshole mode.

"Not gonna lie, Priss," he said the last time I came to the bar for the night. When I continued giving him the cold-shoulder, he leaned toward me as he set the last pitcher on my tray. "You fucking did taste good."

My eyes met his, and hard as I tried to give him my best apathetic look, I knew there was still hurt in them because I saw the concern in his before I spun to deliver my orders hearing him mutter out a "Fuck," as I walked away.

When my shift was finally over, I got the hell out of there as fast as I could and drove home, and in the shower, I cried a bit over what had happened, absolutely hurt about it all. When I went to bed, I lay there thinking about what an ass he was and that was when my phone beeped.

_____

From: 9543254 <student.9543254@hallervan.edu>

Subject: True to form

Date: October 12, 12:26 a.m.

To: 9565876 <student.9565876@hallervan.edu>

Ever make a complete ass of yourself?

Yeah, I have. When I let my guard down with you, I thought as one last tear slipped its way out before I fell asleep.

Week Eight

From: 9543254 <student.9543254@hallervan.edu>

Subject: Quiet

Date: October 17, 11:16 p.m.

To: 9565876 <student.9565876@hallervan.edu>

    Hey

From: 9543254 <student.9543254@hallervan.edu>

Subject: Quiet

Date: October 17, 11:20 p.m.

To: 9565876 <student.9565876@hallervan.edu>

    You around?

From: 9543254 <student.9543254@hallervan.edu>

Subject: Quiet

Date: October 17, 11:41 p.m.

To: 9565876 <student.9565876@hallervan.edu>

    Guess not

From: 9543254 <student.9543254@hallervan.edu>

Subject: Quiet

Date: October 17, 11:59 p.m.

      Six?

From: 9543254 <student.9543254@hallervan.edu>

Subject: Quiet

Date: October 18, 12:09 a.m.

To: 9565876 <student.9565876@hallervan.edu>

      You okay?

From: 9543254 <student.9543254@hallervan.edu>

Subject: Quiet

Date: October 18, 12:15 a.m.

To: 9565876 <student.9565876@hallervan.edu>

      Please answer me when you get this & let me know you're okay

~*~*~*~

I avoided Gable the entire week, coming in late to psych class Monday, Wednesday and Friday just as Dr. Horner had started her lectures, and sat on the front row then left quickly after class before he could approach me. I didn't reply to his emails and I even managed to change shifts with Natalie so I didn't have to work with him.

Maybe this was stupid because it seemed that he and I did nothing but play hide and seek from each other every other week, but I was so angry and hurt about what had happened between us. And it didn't help any that I couldn't stop thinking about that kiss. It'd been so perfect and *he'd* tasted so good and felt so amazing that I couldn't help but want more of him. I'd even woken myself up a couple times, hand between my legs and moaning like a porn star since he'd been starring in my dreams all week. But then I'd remember that it meant nothing to him. That *I* meant nothing to him. I was just the same as all the others before me and that just pissed me off even more.

So knowing all this, I knew I needed to get a grip, let it go and face the fact that he and I would only be friends because I wasn't about to become a member of the Revolving Door Brigade, aka the women that lined up to get a piece of the man himself.

And that made me sadder than sad.

~*~*~*~

"Priss. Long time no talk."

I placed my tray on the bar. It was Friday night and I'd managed to stay out of his path all week. "Yeah, I've been busy." I wasn't going to be hateful to him; why would I when I really did care about him? So I tightened my resolve when he grinned at me and gave him a small smile back.

"Hi, handsome," Alyssa crooned as she stepped up beside me, setting her tray down as she made googly eyes at Gable which made me want to punch her.

He turned and jerked his chin up at her, pretty much blowing her off as he filled her order.

Awkward.

"So, baby, we on for tonight?" she asked him.

He stood at the beer tap and I saw his spine go straight. When he turned and set two beer mugs and a pitcher on the counter, he leaned in and said to her, "I'm not your baby. Look, Alyssa, we had fun a few times. It's run its course. Nothing personal."

She stared at him with her mouth hanging open.

I take it back. *This* was awkward.

I watched her face twist into some demonic entity which made me step away from her then hands on her hips, she leaned right back and spit at him, "You think you're so big and bad, Gable Powers. But let me tell you this, my boyfriend is *so* much better than you! So you can go fuck yourself for all I care!" She picked up her tray and spun around so fast that a new waitress would've spilled everything, but not Alyssa. She was a veteran at this and handled it pretty damned gracefully, I had to say.

I turned and regarded Gable with raised brows only to see his eyes dancing with humor.

"Wow," I mumbled.

He leaned down placing his forearms on the counter getting right up in my face. "That? Huge mistake, Priss. To be honest, I only hit it once and it was done before it was over, and that was two months ago. I also didn't know she had a boyfriend."

I pulled back, looking skeptically at him. I also threw a little indifference in there.

He shrugged. "What can I say? Not lookin' to be tied down. She's hot. Made sense at the time."

I shrugged offhandedly. Why did I care? I was sticking to the "just friends" rule I'd set anyway, so he owed me no explanations whatsoever as far as I was concerned.

He filled my order and helped me put it all on the tray. "So, what're you doing after work?" he asked, his honey eyes locking onto mine and holding me hostage.

I blinked myself out of the Gable-induced stupor I was in and frowned at him wondering what he was up to. "Probably just going home."

"Come out with me," he said.

I huffed out a small laugh of disbelief then shook my head, still frowning. "Gable... I can't..."

"Please? I want to show you something that I think you'd like." And believe it or not, he didn't even turn that statement into anything sexual.

He looked so sincerely at me, so hopeful, that I couldn't help myself. I closed my eyes and took a deep breath. When I opened them, I nodded at him which got me a stellar smile. God. He was something else. "I'll see," I answered. We were friends. Friends did things together, right?

"Good enough," he replied, still smiling.

"And where would we be going?" I asked.

"It's a surprise." He smiled. "You get off at eleven, right?" he inquired.

All I could do was nod again.

"'Kay. I'm supposed to be here until midnight, but we're slow and I'm sure Uncle Jack won't mind if Aaron covers for me. Think you could stick around until eleven-fifteen?"

"I guess." I hoped I wasn't being a huge pushover, but, again, it wasn't like we couldn't be friends.

I reached to pick up my tray and he grabbed my hand. The cliché spark between us was still there and my eyes slid up to his to see him looking at me as if he was trying to convey several messages to me at once, maybe, *I'm sorry.* Or, *You're different than the other girls. Give me a chance to prove it to you.* Or maybe I was hoping that was what he was trying to say.

Not lookin' to be tied down.

That. That right there told me I was delusional and he wanted nothing more than to hang out, so I gave him another small smile then picked up my tray, heading to my tables to fill orders, all the while knowing what I'd read in his eyes had only been what I wanted to see.

So I pulled up my big-girl panties and put to rest any thoughts that Gable and I would ever be anything more than friends.

~*~*~*~

I was sitting in a daze wrapping silverware mooning over what had occurred earlier when I'd come back here to perform the mundane chore. I'd gone to grab more napkins when I'd seen the most spectacular thing ever. Gable had been in the bathroom with the door open changing his shirt, and holy God I almost hyperventilated. Good lord, the man was hot. I saw that his pecs were sculpted and defined and magnificent. Then there were his abs that were absolutely amazing, so cut and defined and I swear I drooled a little as I watched him. And all of that hadn't even been the coup de grâce. His entire chest was covered in tattoos, a colorful conglomeration of patterns and designs that I knew right then and there that I wanted to spend hours studying, gazing upon and licking every last bit of each. I'd continued staring as his biceps bunched beautifully as he pulled on another shirt, my mouth hanging open in awe. When he'd turned to see me looking at him, he gave me a lazy smirk then slowly closed the door. Its click brought me out of my trance and realizing I'd been gawking at him, my face instantly heated. Shit. I immediately grabbed the napkins and got the heck out of there, mentally reprimanding myself for being such a sucker for a hot body and forgetting my vow not to think of him carnally. Ugh.

"Ready?"

I jumped when Gable whispered in my ear from behind bringing me out my musings of seeing him half-naked. I turned to tell him I'd be ready in a minute but his face was still right there so that our cheeks brushed and I felt his light scruff against my skin. If I turned just a bit more, our lips would be touching. At that alarming thought, I moved away from him quickly, standing up from the stool I'd been sitting on to wrap silverware, almost knocking it over. God. I had to stop letting him get me off balance all the time.

"Yeah, give me a minute," I replied between gritted teeth, angry at myself for being such a fool for him, as I placed my last roll of utensils in the bin. I then glanced down at the half jersey I wore. "I'd really like to change first."

"Okay," he answered with a nod, helping me on with my coat that I'd grabbed from the hook on the back wall. "You want me to follow you to your place so you can change then you can ride with me?"

Hm. Did I want him to know where I lived? I stood there thinking about that and biting my lip for so long he finally took my hand and led me out the back. He walked me to my car and after I dug my keys out of my purse I looked up at him.

"I'll be right behind you," he said then waited for me to get in my car and start it before he jogged to his.

I glanced in my rearview mirror several times as he followed me, wondering what the hell the evening held for me and if I was being a dumbass. "Just friends," I reminded myself as I pulled up to my apartment, parking and opening my door to see that he was already there holding his hand out to me. I took it guardedly and got out then he shut my door behind me. As we walked toward my apartment, I tried taking my hand from his but he held strong, not letting mine go; therefore, I was internally freaking out because I knew Amy would die if she saw it and would probably say something inappropriate, embarrassing the hell out of me. And God forbid if Bodhi was over. He'd probably ask Gable out himself.

Since I hadn't seen either of their cars in the lot, I was hoping I was in the clear, yet I knew stranger things had happened. And since it was a Friday night, I knew Amy wouldn't be in bed. I was praying that she was out with friends and not inside drinking beer and debating with Bodhi as I warily put the key into the lock. But when I opened the door, to my relief, the apartment was empty and I let out a huge breath.

"You okay?" Gable asked with a chuckle as we walked inside. "Got a jealous husband you were hoping wasn't here or something?" He raised an eyebrow as he looked at me.

I chuckled. "No. I was just hoping my roommate wasn't here." He kept the eyebrow up and I explained. "Well, you're *you* and everyone knows who you and your brothers are." As he still kept his eyes on me, I continued. "She'd give me shit about it then wanna hold a three-hour Q and A session. I just didn't feel up to it tonight."

He frowned but nodded as if he understood, studying me like he was trying to figure me out which wasn't a little unsettling.

"I'll just, uh, go change. Make yourself comfortable. Not sure what's in the fridge, but if you're thirsty, I'm sure you can find something." He nodded and I left him in the living room, heading to my room and closing the door once inside. I then grabbed my phone out of my pocket. "Hey," I said quietly when Amy picked up. "Gable's here and he's taking me somewhere but won't tell me where," I whispered.

I listened first of all to her scream over loud music, suddenly remembering that she and Bodhi had planned to go to out tonight. Amy had met a guy named Chad in the library a while back and they'd been flirting for the past couple weeks and now she and Bodhi were at his place for some bash he was throwing. I'd really wanted to meet him but work had made me miss out. Now I heard her inform Bodhi of what was going on, then he was suddenly on the line asking excitedly, "Gable Powers is at your apartment?"

"Yeah. Don't get your panties in a twist. We're just friends," I reminded him.

"Yeah, but he likes you, Scout. I know he wants more with you."

"How can you know that, Bodhi?" I mean, I really wanted to know. Bodhi was a guy. He'd know this stuff.

"Because he's trying. If you were just someone he wanted to fuck, do you think he'd even be giving you the time of day?"

I thought about that for a moment but felt it wasn't enough. Hm. Bodhi was really falling down on his dude intuition. "Well, he just said earlier that he wasn't looking to be tied down. So, again, we're just *friends*."

"Friends schmeinds! And I'm sure he'd love to be tied down by you." He giggled maniacally at this making me roll my eyes. "Have fun! Don't do anything I wouldn't do!" I heard his voice fade then Amy came on the line.

"Don't listen to him, Scout. Do everything. That boy's hot!" She giggled a little drunkenly.

"How's the party?" I asked.

"God, Scout! Chad's so hot!" she squealed.

"Good! You think it could get serious with you two?"

"Maybe! I think he's gonna be my next ex-boyfriend!"

I snorted out a laugh. "You're crazy. Okay, have fun and call me if you need a ride."

"Bodhi's friend Max is with us and he's the DD, so we're good. But you have fun too! Full details later!"

"Same!" I said before the line went dead.

I scrambled around finding a shirt to put on then changed my jeans finally hustling out of my room to the bathroom where I fixed my hair a bit, put on more lip gloss and spritzed myself with some body spray. When I came out and walked into the living room, I saw Gable looking at pictures Amy and I had just put up on the wall. I walked to him then just about died. The collage of pictures was of us from when we were little girls to now. I'd had Dad text me a few pictures, one of which was of me driving our tractor when I was younger and Gable was now staring at it.

"That you?" he asked, pointing at the photo.

I stared at it and cleared my throat. "Yeah." God, he had to know now.

I could feel him watching me out of the corner of his eye as I waited for him to yell at me, but then he asked, "Ready?"

Well, he was either an extremely good actor or just plain naïve. How many more clues did the guy need?

"Yeah..." He took my hand and led me outside where I locked the apartment door then we walked to his car and he did the whole seatbelt thing again which at once thrilled me and annoyed me.

"Might wanna get this fixed," I mumbled as he leaned over me buckling me in. I mean, not that I minded, but it was going to be hard to just be friends when he was *right there* within lip locking distance.

He chuckled. "Yeah." He moved away and shut my door, and as I watched him walking around to get in his side, I realized that he was doing an incredible job of keeping his distance, probably trying to show me he was interested in me as a person and not just for sex, which I had to admit

I suddenly found rather irritating and I huffed out a small laugh thinking I just couldn't be satisfied.

When Gable got in, I asked, "Now will you tell me where we're going?"

He grinned. "You'll see."

He started the car and "Cry of Achilles" by Alter Bridge blared from his speakers until he reached quickly to turn it down. What the hell? He'd said in his first email that he didn't really like them!

"Alter Bridge?" I asked, shocked.

He glanced over at me with a sexy half grin. "Yeah."

"My favorite band."

He glanced at me again. "Yeah?"

I nodded a couple times again still wondering if he knew. Ugh. All this tiptoeing around shit was driving me nutso. If I didn't end up in the loony bin by the end of the semester, I'd be surprised. But I let it go and we made small talk as he drove, ignoring the obvious, or at least I was. Ten minutes later we pulled into a parking lot near an old building.

When I looked at him a little confused, he explained, "Midnight movies."

Awesome! I couldn't help the smile that came to my face. "Really? I love movies!"

He smiled back then got out, coming around to my side and opening the door. As he worked on getting my seatbelt off, he said, "Saw your column in the paper and thought you might like this."

He saw my column and thought I'd like this place. That was seriously the sweetest thing ever. And despite the "Just friends" mantra I had running through my head, I now wondered how the hell I was supposed to rein in my feelings for him when what I wanted to do was jump his bones for being so thoughtful. He held his hand out for me to take, helping me out of his car and I caved, tiptoeing up to kiss his cheek. His arms immediately went around my waist and he pulled me into a tight hug, burying his face into my hair at the side of my neck as he let out a deep sigh like he was relieved that I'd forgiven him.

God. How was I supposed to deal with this? I took a deep breath of my own and letting it out, made myself pull away from him as my conscience screamed, *JUST FRIENDS!* inside my head. I gave him a smile then turned to face the theater. "What's showing?" I asked as we started walking toward the old building.

"*Casablanca*." He took my hand again, smoothing his thumb over the back of mine as we walked.

One of my favorites. Huh. Did he know he was killing me slowly with *everything* right now?

Once inside, we found our seats but then he told me he'd be right back. While he was gone, I inspected the theater, admiring the antique-looking sconces on the walls and the arched ceiling that was separated in panels and painted with various scenes from famous movies. Very cool.

Gable came back holding a bucket of popcorn and two soft drinks. Oh, he was really pushing it with all the niceness now.

"I hope you like Milk Duds," he said when he sat down, handing me a soda and putting the popcorn bucket on his thigh so I could reach it.

"Unfortunately for my ass, I happen to love Milk Duds, especially with popcorn," I replied with a chuckle.

"Ah, Priss, you know what I think about your ass," he said, wiggling his eyebrows and making me blush which made my resistance flag for a minute.

Just friends!

Before I could reply, the theater lights blinked off and on then the movie started. And everything was fine until halfway through when he reached over and took my hand, bringing it to his lips for a small kiss before he rested our clasped hands on his thigh and my heart melted.

~*~*~*~

Two hours later, we sat in an all-night coffee house discussing the movie.

"I would've stayed with Rick," I said. "I just don't know how Ilsa could leave him." I took a bite of the amazing Danish pastry I'd ordered.

"She was married to Victor," Gable replied, eyebrow raised and pointing his own pastry at me when he said that.

"Well, yeah. But I think everyone has that someone... well, that someone who makes the stitches worth it, and Rick was hers." I shrugged a shoulder.

"Stitches?" he asked, his eyes narrowing on mine.

Well, crap. I'd revealed something to him that I didn't share with too many people.

When we were in high school, Ivy and I had sat up one night talking about love, and I'd told her it was like having someone rip your chest open, take your heart out and hold it in their hand as they tore off pieces of it. Then they returned it and stitched you back up. I'd finished by saying that only a few people were worthy of your stitches. She'd frowned at me like I was crazy, but that's exactly how I thought love felt. I'd told her that it made your heart hurt even if it was good. She hadn't understood and I hadn't tried expounding any further. If someone didn't get it, they never would.

"It's kind of silly," I responded sheepishly.

"Tell me, Priss." His eyes looked curiously at me.

So with a sigh, I explained my theory to him while he listened intently.

When I finished, I said shyly, "Stupid, huh?" I glanced down at my coffee waiting for him to laugh at me.

"Not at all. I get it."

I looked up at him to see if he was playing with me but when I saw that he was serious, I asked carefully, "You've had stitches?"

"Yeah..." he answered, shifting in his chair and seeming a little uncomfortable.

"Don't wanna talk about it," I said.

He ran a hand over his mouth, his fingers then going to his chin to scratch the scruff that was there. "It's not something I typically discuss." I looked thoughtfully at him wondering what or who could've hurt him. I nodded in acceptance of his answer but was surprised when he continued. "Let's just say I got hurt. By her and..." He looked at me so conflicted, the hurt showing clearly in his eyes as his hand went to the back of his neck to rub it, that I just wanted to give him a hug. "By her and, a, uh, friend."

I blinked as I watched him, somewhat surprised that he'd shared that much with me.

He pursed his lips. "Reason why I'll never have 'stitches' again," he mumbled almost as if to himself as he looked down at his drink he was spinning slowly on the table in his fingers. We stayed silent for a bit but when he finally looked up at me, I knew the moment had passed if the shit-eating grin on his face was any indication. "Wouldn't mind lookin' at your stitches, though."

I huffed out a laugh. "God, every time I think you're normal, you never fail to remind me that you're an asshole."

I watched as his grin got bigger then he shrugged as if to say, "Mission accomplished."

All I could do was shake my head as I chuckled. "So, I should probably get back. Make sure Amy's okay and not puking her guts out." It was two-thirty, so I thought she'd probably be home from the party unless she'd decided to take things to the next level and stay with Chad.

Gable nodded then stood and held a hand out, helping me out of the booth. Dang. He'd certainly learned somewhere how to be a gentleman. I let him hold my hand on the way to his car telling myself not to put too much into it because I knew if I did, he'd only hurt me in the end.

He was so quiet on the way to my apartment I asked if he was okay.

"Yeah. Just thinking," he answered.

I knew my stitches theory had opened up old wounds for him which made me feel kind of bad for bringing it up.

When we got to my apartment, he came around to unbuckle me and help me out of the car. "Thank you for going with me," he said after walking me to my door.

"Thank you for taking me," I said with a smile.

He looked down at me as if trying to make a decision, so I made it for him by tiptoeing up and kissing his cheek again. "Good night," I said before unlocking the door and going inside, watching him walk to his car before I closed the door.

I went to Amy's room to see if she was there, which she was, so I guessed she was holding off on making Chad her next ex, which made me chuckle quietly. Her soft snores indicated that she was fine, so I slowly closed her door and walked back into the living room then heard a low knock on the front door. I went to it and through the eyehole saw it was Gable and I frowned wondering what he'd forgotten.

"Hey," I said when I opened the door. He was standing with his arms raised above him, his hands holding onto the top of the door frame and he looked at me for a beat, his eyes narrowed on mine, before he stepped inside quickly and, taking my face in his hands, bent down and smashed his mouth to mine proceeding to give me the kiss of a lifetime. I was stunned for a few seconds but recovered quickly, bringing my arms up to lace around his neck and tangling my fingers into his hair as the kiss got deeper and hotter. Whoa. He somehow ended up inside the apartment, kicking the door closed behind him, then turned us, backing me against it and pressing the hard planes of his body into my soft ones. His hands slid down and cupped my butt before he picked me up making me wrap my legs around his waist, and, sweet Jesus, I knew right then all my inner babblings of encouragement to stay the hell away from him were wasted because in that moment I wanted him more than I wanted my next breath.

We made out for what seemed like *ever*, which was totally amazing, and the instant I was so thoroughly worked up that I was ready to lead him to my bedroom where I could have my wicked way with him, he pulled away, and resting his forehead against mine, gazed down at me and muttered, "Fuck," then touched his mouth to mine briefly, set my feet back on the floor, kissed my forehead, said, "Good night, Scout," and was out the door and gone before I could even catch my breath.

I leaned back against the closed door, throwing my head back to bang against it as I looked up at the ceiling. Oh, Gable, how you excite me, thrill me, and totally, completely and thoroughly confuse me.

Week Nine

From: 9565876 <student.9565876@hallervan.edu>

Subject: Sorry

Date: October 22, 3:52 p.m.

To: 9543254 <student.9543254@hallervan.edu>

Dear Mr. Four,

I just wanted you to know I'm okay. I've just been busy. Sorry I made you worry.

Hope last week & this week were awesome & your classes are going great!

Just a question... if someone knew something about you but didn't tell you, what would you do?

Six

xo

From: 9543254 <student.9543254@hallervan.edu>

Subject: Sorry

Date: October 22, 4:02 p.m.

To: 9565876 <student.9565876@hallervan.edu>

Mr. Four. I like it.

Glad you're okay. Thanks for letting me know. I was worried.

Classes are good, some better than others.

Hm. If someone knew something about me and didn't tell me? I'd think of it as lying and, well, I hate liars. I can't help it, but I hold grudges, so if someone lies to me, I'm pretty much finished with them. Why?

xx

~*~*~*~

Shit. Would Gable think my knowing he was my pen pal and not telling him was a lie? I was afraid to find out because I didn't want to lose his friendship or whatever this was that we had going.

In "real life" things had been going great with him. He'd sat by me Monday and Wednesday in psych class. He'd held my hand when we walked out then given me a sweet kiss before I went to my next class both days. This weekend we were going on a ghost tour of Seattle, which I was really excited about, especially since Halloween was just around the corner. On top of all that, he'd asked for my number and we'd begun texting. So now I not only had to keep up with him through email, I had to deal with texting him too. The double life I was living with him was weighing on me and I didn't know how much longer I could keep it up without spilling it all. It was too confusing trying to remember what I'd told him through emails and in person, so I'd made the decision that I'd be more distant in my emails, thinking that'd solve things.

I should've known it wouldn't.

~*~*~*~

From: 9543254 <student.9543254@hallervan.edu>

Subject: Can't take it

Date: October 22, 11:09 p.m.

To: 9565876 <student.9565876@hallervan.edu>

Six,

I fantasize about you. Can't get you out of my head...

From: 9565876 <student.9565876@hallervan.edu>

Subject: Are YOU drunk?

Date: October 22, 11:34 p.m.

To: 9543254 <student.9543254@hallervan.edu>

Um...

From: 9543254 <student.9543254@hallervan.edu>

Subject: Perfectly sober...

Date: October 22, 11:35 p.m.

To: 9565876 <student.9565876@hallervan.edu>

I want to taste your lips... want to touch you... want to be with you...

~*~*~*~

Holy shit. He was being really bold in his emails and I wasn't sure what to do about it. On the one hand, what he was saying was flattering, not to mention hot, but on the other, if he didn't know I was his pen pal and he was writing those things to a girl he thought he didn't know, well, then that was just a giant hole of suck.

"You should just tell him who you are," Bodhi said Thursday at lunch.

"You think? I mean, this has grown into some huge fucking monster now." I shook my head at how absurd it'd all become. "If I tell him, he'll think I was lying this whole time and hate me."

Bodhi stuffed half of his generic Pizza Pocket into his mouth, chewed twice and downed it. I'd never understand how the guy could stay so skinny when he ate as much as a herd of elephants. He threw the last half of it in his mouth and said between chews, "He couldn't hate you. He likes you."

I frowned. "I forwarded the email to you. You saw what he said about lying." I took a drink from my bottle of water. This was making me miserable, even to the point that I felt guilty for having fun when Gable and I were together.

Bodhi drank the rest of his soda. "Yeah, but I still don't think it'd change his mind."

I just shook my head and rolled my eyes because I thought it would.

"You could just pretend when you guys do the reveal that you didn't know it was him and act all surprised."

"Yeah, and that surely wouldn't be a lie, would it?" I answered sarcastically.

Bodhi shrugged. "Don't know what else to tell you. Sorry, Scout."

"Thanks anyway, Bode," I mumbled, watching as he put all his trash on his tray.

He stood then bent to kiss me on the forehead. "It'll be okay. Promise." He picked up his tray and left for his next class.

I hoped he was right.

~*~*~*~

Text Message—Thurs, Oct 24, 11:34 p.m.

Gable: What're you doing?

Me: Studying, as usual

Gable: You're so dedicated

Me: Gotta keep the scholarship ;)

Gable: I know. Hey, remember when I told you about Justin asking my dad about that part he needed for his car?

Me: Yes

Gable: Yeah. He lied to my dad and said I told him he could pick it up for free. He came by the shop this morning and got it. Dad called and asked what was going on. So I called Justin and he fucking lied to me about it saying Dad gave it to him. Told him I knew he was lying and was done with him.

Me: But you've been friends for, what, fifteen years?

Gable: I don't give a shit. He lied. That's not cool. He told me he was sorry and everything but that's one thing I can't stand is a liar. Fuck him. I don't need that shit in my life.

Great. He'd ended a fifteen-year relationship and all because the guy lied. I was so screwed.

Gable: *Ready for tomorrow night?*

Me: *Yes! I love ghost stuff!*

Gable: *I'm kinda fascinated by it too*

Me: *What if we get attacked by a poltergeist or something?*

Gable: *You HAVE seen those ghost hunter shows, right? Nothing ever gets them*

Me: *Oh, something definitely gets ME 'cause that one has a really hot guy who's the head ghost hunter...*

Gable: *Huh...*

Me: *What? You want me to tell you he's not as hot as you?*

Gable: *That'd be nice*

Me: *Oh, Gable, you're SO much hotter than that Zac guy! He doesn't even begin to compare to you... your tattoos are way better than his... you're so much stronger than he is... I'll bet you can out-ghost him any day*

Gable: *Smartass. He has tattoos?*

Me: *Yep*

Gable: *Hm. That's cool. Hey, what if you get possessed or something and start spewing pea soup?*

Me: *I'd be possessed to knock your block off...*

Gable: *That'd be cool too*

Me: *It can be arranged*

Gable: Know what?

Me: What?

Gable: You're cute

Me: Okay, I have to call you hot but you call me cute?

Gable: Oh, you're hot too… but you're also cute

Me: I think I'm blushing

Gable: I can do some things to you that'll make you blush

Me: Now I know I'm blushing

Gable: Can't wait to see you tomorrow… want to taste your lips…

All right, now, seriously, I didn't know whether to be thrilled or pissed that he was telling me the same things he was telling his pen pal. God. I was totally losing it by being jealous about myself.

Me: I love your lips on mine…

Gable: I'd love my lips anywhere on you…

Me: Wow…

Gable: Your lips… neck… shoulder…

Me: Wait. Are we sexting?

Gable: Only if you want to be

Me: Well, I really need to go put a load of laundry in

Gable: Chicken…

Me: I'm embarrassed

Gable: Nothing to be embarrassed about... it's just me

Me: I know. Give me some time to get used to this?

Gable: Yeah. K, go do your laundry xx

Me: See you tomorrow xo

I didn't really have to do laundry. I really was a chicken.

After brushing my teeth and just as I lay down in bed, my phone alerted me that I had an email.

From: 9543254 <student.9543254@hallervan.edu>

Subject: You

Date: October 25, 12:03 a.m.

To: 9565876 <student.9565876@hallervan.edu>

Six,

Seriously can't get you off my mind...

xx

Damn it. Now it felt as if he were cheating on me by emailing *her*. Who was *me*. But I didn't know if he knew it. Arrgggghhh!

From: 9565876 <student.9565876@hallervan.edu>

Subject: You

Date: October 25, 12:05 a.m.

To: 9543254 <student.9543254@hallervan.edu>

Mr. Four,

Why?

xo

From: 9543254 <student.9543254@hallervan.edu>

Subject: You

Date: October 25, 12:07 a.m.

To: 9565876 <student.9565876@hallervan.edu>.

I don't know. I can't stop thinking about you.

xx

From: 9565876 <student.9565876@hallervan.edu>

Subject: You

Date: October 25, 12:07 a.m.

To: 9543254 <student.9543254@hallervan.edu>

You don't really even know me

From: 9543254 <student.9543254@hallervan.edu>

Subject: You

Date: October 25, 12:08 a.m.

To: 9565876 <student.9565876@hallervan.edu>

I know, but I want to

xx

From: 9565876 <student.9565876@hallervan.edu>

Subject: You

Date: October 25, 12:08 a.m.

To: 9543254 <student.9543254@hallervan.edu>

Maybe after we meet at the end of the semester?

From: 9543254 <student.9543254@hallervan.edu>

Subject: You

Date: October 25, 12:09 a.m.

To: 9565876 <student.9565876@hallervan.edu>

I want to fuck you

xx

Holy Moses. There he went with his escalating quickly bit again.

As the shock wore off, once again, I couldn't figure out if I should be jealous or not. I mean, here he'd just tried to sext *real* me and now he was suggesting intercourse via Internet with *pen pal* me. I really hoped he knew I was both. Ugh.

As I thought about it, I figured I could go one of two ways with this. I could ignore him now and when I next emailed him I'd just keep things at an impersonal level and not egg him on. Or I could go for it. I mean, what would it hurt, well, other than real me if he was really into pen pal me and didn't know I was her.

God, I was one sick bitch.

My curiosity won and I moved forward thinking that when he found out at semester's end that it was me he'd been writing and that I'd basically lied to him and he never wanted to see me again, at least I'd had a little fun with it, right?

Yeah. A little fun and a ton of heartbreak.

I took a deep breath and replied.

From: 9565876 <student.9565876@hallervan.edu>

Subject: You

Date: October 25, 12:15 a.m.

To: 9543254 <student.9543254@hallervan.edu>

I don't think I'd be opposed to that...

xo

EEP!

From: 9543254 <student.9543254@hallervan.edu>

Subject: You

Date: October 25, 12:15 a.m.

To: 9565876 <student.9565876@hallervan.edu>

Baby, I'd make you so hot, opposition would be the farthest thing from your mind... you'd be begging for more

---

From: 9565876 <student.9565876@hallervan.edu>

Subject: You

Date: October 25, 12:15 a.m.

To: 9543254 <student.9543254@hallervan.edu>

Tell me…

From: 9543254 <student.9543254@hallervan.edu>

Subject: You

Date: October 25, 12:16 a.m.

To: 9565876 <student.9565876@hallervan.edu>

First I'd kiss you so hot and deep your head would spin… my fingers in your hair… your arms around my neck… I'd kiss your jaw… down your neck… in the hollow of your throat… then I'd take your shirt off… your bra… and see your gorgeous tits… I'd suck on your nipples… make you come just from that…

Oh, my God.

This was hot.

Gable didn't mess around.

When I was with Hayden, his emails had been amateur compared. Good lord. Suddenly, I wasn't so sure I was up to this. I'd always been the bold one with Hayden but Gable had taken this to a whole other level.

I took a deep breath, gave myself a sex pep talk, took another deep breath and forged ahead hoping I could keep up with him.

From: 9565876 <student.9565876@hallervan.edu>

Subject: You

Date: October 25, 12:18 a.m.

To: 9543254 <student.9543254@hallervan.edu>

Oh, God, I love that… I'd wrap my fingers in your hair, knowing you'd make me come… I'd be so wet for you… I'd take off your shirt to see your strong, muscular chest… run my tongue all over your pecs, bite your nipples lightly… tease you with my tongue as I ran it down over your abs…

Subject: You

Date: October 25, 12:21 a.m.

To: 9565876 <student.9565876@hallervan.edu>

God, that's hot as fuck, Six...

Next, I'd lay you on my bed then take your jeans off... see you in your sexy panties... then pull them down your legs and off... kiss up the inside of your thighs until I got to your beautiful pussy, then I'd kiss you there... run my tongue all over you... taste your sweetness going down my throat... fuck you with my tongue... then when I had you panting, right where I wanted you, I'd suck your clit and I'd fucking love it when you screamed my name as you came harder than you ever have... harder than you came the first time...

Wow.

From: 9565876 <student.9565876@hallervan.edu>

Subject: You

Date: October 25, 12:24 a.m.

To: 9543254 <student.9543254@hallervan.edu>

God... you make me so hot... I'd unzip your jeans and reach in and pull your big cock out then worship it with my tongue next... licking it from bottom to top, my hand cupping your balls... making you groan for more... I'd take the head into my mouth and suck... then I'd take all of you in my mouth, going down on you until you touched the back of my throat... then I'd slide my mouth up, sucking your rock hard cock until I got to the tip then twirling my tongue around it I'd look at you watching me suck you off as I moved my lips back down again...

From: 9543254 <student.9543254@hallervan.edu>

Subject: You

Date: October 25, 12:27 a.m.

To: 9565876 <student.9565876@hallervan.edu>

Jesus... I want to fuck you so bad right now... I'd grab you under your arms and pull you up to me, kissing you again hard then turn over with you underneath me... pull your leg up, holding it behind your knee then I'd thrust my cock inside you so fucking hard, you'd scream my name as you came again... God, I'd fuck you so fucking hard... driving inside that sweet pussy of yours over and over... turn you on your stomach and fuck you from behind... going so fucking deep making you moan each time I thrust inside you...

Fuck, Six... I'm gonna go fucking jack off in the bathroom now...

I sat there panting wanting him to do everything to me that he'd just said.

Then I realized what I'd done. Crap. There really wasn't any going back from this now. I mean, how the hell could we just have casual conversations through email any more? Damn it. What was I thinking?

With a shaky hand, I put my phone on my nightstand and tried going to sleep, but the picture of us that Gable had created was too damned hot, so slipping my hand inside my panties, I made myself come, and, believe me, it didn't take long. As I lay there breathing hard my phone beeped again.

From: 9543254 <student.9543254@hallervan.edu>

Subject: You

Date: October 25, 12:40 a.m.

To: 9565876 <student.9565876@hallervan.edu>

Six, I have to meet you. The Sig Eps are having their masked Halloween party next Thursday. Can you be there?

xx

Okay, the party could be the perfect opportunity to let him know I was his pen pal. If he got mad when he found out, it'd give him time to get over it by second semester. But what if he wasn't only mad, he was disappointed? God. That would be devastating.

As I hit "Reply," I smacked myself in the head knowing I'd dug myself into a deep, deep hole. I so should've told him it was me when I found out I was writing to him in the first place.

From: 9565876 <student.9565876@hallervan.edu>

Subject: You

Date: October 25, 12:44 a.m.

To: 9543254 <student.9543254@hallervan.edu>

Um, maybe. If I can get my roommate to go, I'll be there.

xo

From: 9543254 <student.9543254@hallervan.edu>

Subject: You

Date: October 25, 12:46 a.m.

To: 9565876 <student.9565876@hallervan.edu>

Good. I need to see you...

xx

~*~*~*~

"Are you free on Halloween?" I asked Amy the next morning.

She glanced up from where she sat at the table, elbow propped on it and head in her hand as she ate her cereal. She wasn't a morning person by any means. "Probably." She yawned. "Why?" she asked, slurping a spoonful of Cheerios into her mouth.

"Pen pal Gable asked me to the Sig Eps' Halloween party and I told him I'd go if you went with me." I gave her my winningest smile.

"Pen pal Gable. So *real* Gable still doesn't know it's you he's emailing but you're going out with him in real life, and now he wants to meet pen pal you. Do I have this right?" The look she shot me unmistakably relayed that she thought I was a moron. I think I heard her mutter that I was so fucked but I didn't ask her to repeat herself because I knew she was right.

I sat down at the table and sighed. "I know it's stupid, but I really like him and I think he really likes me and he wants to meet me at this party."

"*Me* as in pen pal you."

I nodded. Yep. She was right. This was totally crazy.

"Scout, you know if he doesn't know it's you and he finds out it's you, all hell could break loose, right?"

Amy and I had talked about this several times and true to form, she had the opposite opinion of Bodhi. While he was encouraging saying that Gable wouldn't be mad, Amy thought he'd be pissed and end it all. She and Bodhi had even had a knock-down-drag-out over it a couple nights before which had made me wholly uncomfortable that their topic of debate had been the direction my relationship status with Gable would take when things finally came to a head. I hadn't even been able to yell at them to stop because they both had valid points.

"I know." I looked at her sheepishly as I buttered my bagel. "But look at it this way. Even though I'm pretty sure he knows it's me, at least it'll all finally be over and we'll know who won between you and Bodhi in the great 'Scout is a dumbass' debate."

She sighed as she scooped another spoonful into her mouth. After swallowing, she said, "I just don't want to see you get hurt. But I'll go with you to pick up the pieces if it doesn't pan out. Besides, Chad said something about going." She shrugged as she focused on eating her cereal. Definitely not a morning person.

I thanked her and as I sat eating my bagel, I couldn't help thinking how screwed up everything was. When I finished, I went to my room to get dressed for class but couldn't even be happy that Amy had agreed to go with me because just talking about it had made my stomach churn.

~*~*~*~

That night Gable and I went on the ghost tour which had been a blast. It'd been more of a historical expedition than a haunted one, but I loved history too, so it was still fascinating to hear the stories.

"I remember being scared shitless when my dad had taken my brothers and me on this when we were little," he whispered to me as the guide told us about a building that had once been a brothel. "Nice. Haunted whores," Gable murmured which made me elbow him in the side as I giggled quietly. "Priss, what more could a man want? Faceless chick giving you head for free?"

I elbowed him even harder that time, making him utter an "Oomph!" not bothering to laugh as I remembered our sexy email exchange, not knowing if he was hinting that he knew I was the faceless chick who'd been writing to him about giving him head or if I was just reading more into what he said. God, I'd be so glad when this semester was over and he knew.

After the tour, we stopped at an espresso bar with many of the others that'd been in our group.

"So?" he asked as we walked back to his car, sipping on his drink. I looked up at him in question before taking a drink of my latte. "What'd you think? Were you scared?"

"Only of the company I was keeping," I said dryly.

He choked out a laugh. "Damn, Scout. That's harsh."

Not being able to keep my cynical attitude going, I laughed with him. "Kidding. But, yes, it was fun. I learned more about Seattle than I ever cared to know."

He laughed again then threw his arm across my shoulders and pulled me to him, his forearm crossing over my throat as he held me close to him as we walked. "Someone's wanting a spanking," he mumbled in my ear making me shiver for some damned reason. I knew he felt it when he chuckled into my hair then he kissed the side of my head, then moving his forearm from my throat to where his hand cupped the side of my shoulder, we continued walking to his car, sipping our drinks as we went.

"Thank you for taking me tonight," I told him when we pulled up to my apartment.

"My pleasure, Priss," he replied with a sexy smile as he turned off the car. Then he leaned over and kissed me softly, but as with all our kisses, things heated up quickly. He pulled back and unbuckled his seatbelt as I messed with mine until he ended up having to take over. As soon as I was out of it, I launched myself at him practically pushing him back into his door.

Oh, damn. I could kiss this man for days.

He scooted around a bit before pulling me into his lap to where I was straddling him in his seat, our mouths never leaving each other's, and when his hands slid under my sweater gliding smoothly across my back where he wrapped one around my waist and the other made its way up and out of the neck where his fingers twisted in my hair, I couldn't even find it in me to care that he was probably stretching it out. I only knew I wanted him. Oh, God, I wanted him so badly.

"Come inside. Stay with me tonight," I mumbled against his lips, after many hot, wet, deep, panty-melting kisses later.

"Can't," he muttered back, hands on my hips and pulling me down to grind against the considerable bulge in his jeans which made me gasp and want him that much more. "But let me make you come."

Before I could say a word, maybe ask him why he couldn't stay with me, he moved back and lifted my sweater in the front with one hand, yanking one of the cups of my bra down with the other then his hot mouth was on my me, sucking my nipple in, making me cry out loudly, my hands on his head holding him to me, my fingers twisting in his hair pulling hard. When he moved to my other breast doing the same, I threw a hand out, hitting the window and noticed it was fogged over and I'd left a handprint on it.

Oh, man.

He leaned back and pulled my sweater up and over my head and off, throwing it into the passenger seat, and when he turned back, he froze, sitting still for several seconds, his eyes scanning every last bit of skin of mine he'd exposed.

"My God, Scout." His eyes languidly made their way to mine, the whiskey color flaring in them as they burned into mine. "You're stunning." His hand went to the back of my head where his fingers tangled in my hair and he pulled me down into a hotter than hot kiss.

"Gable," I said breathily against his mouth when I felt his other hand at the fly of my jeans, tugging on buttons then his hand was inside, his fingers expertly moving over me, and when he pushed aside my panties and slid a finger inside, I cried out.

"So fucking sweet," he said leaning in and taking a nipple into his mouth before moving his way up to my neck, nipping, sucking, licking and tasting along the way. When he pressed his thumb in circling it against me and then his finger started moving inside me, I couldn't help myself as my hips started moving and I rode his hand.

"Jesus, Scout," he said gruffly against my throat, pulling back to watch me as I sought my release.

I glanced down at him and saw he was looking at me as if he wanted to devour me, and even though he'd told me he couldn't stay with me for whatever reason, I wanted that, wanted him to want me. And the look in his eyes said he did.

And that's all it took.

I threw my head back and arched my back when it hit, my fingers digging into his shoulders as a million hot spikes of pleasure claimed every inch of my body and I gasped out his name.

Holy wow.

When my head came forward and I collapsed against him, he wrapped his arms tightly around me and whispered, "Sexiest fucking thing I've ever seen," into my ear as he smoothed my hair down my back with his hand.

My breathing finally slowed and while this was happening my senses also returned. It was then I realized what'd just occurred.

Oh, my God. How embarrassing.

Pulling back slowly from him, I felt the blush coming to my cheeks and as I bit my lip I refused to look at him.

"Hey," he said softly, squeezing my hips with his hands.

I couldn't look at him. Wouldn't. What kind of judgmental bitch was I to think badly of the women who'd thrown themselves at him when here I was having done the same damned thing, naked from the waist up sitting in his lap, still breathing hard from the exceptionally amazing orgasm he'd just given me? I was such a hypocrite. I kept my eyes fixed to the side until he took my chin and gently turned me to look at him. When my eyes finally met his, I sucked in a breath. Oh, my. There was so much emotion in those honey-colored eyes of his it blew me away.

"Hey," he said again. "Fucking perfect, Scout. You're," his hand holding my chin moved to the back of my head and he pulled me down to him, kissing me lightly. "Fucking," he kissed me again. "Perfect." The kiss then got hotter, deeper, wetter, going from sweet to sweltering in a matter of seconds and I realized he was still hard under me which made me moan and grind down on him again.

The guttural sound he expelled against my neck almost made me come again as I moved my hips forward and back over the hard bulge under his jeans, instinct, I guess, or really just me, wanting, needing, aching to have him inside my body.

"Gable," I murmured. "Please."

And then it was over.

He stilled the movement of my hips with his hands, pulling his mouth from my neck and sitting back against his seat. I looked down to see his eyes closed.

"Come inside with me," I whispered, gazing at his beautiful face.

He breathed in slowly through his nose then let it out. "Can't," he stated flatly, his eyes still closed.

Rejected twice in less than thirty minutes. Wow.

I moved off his lap, settling back in the passenger seat as I righted my bra then grabbed my sweater, pulling it on over my head then sat there for several seconds chewing on my lip as I tried to figure out what was going on. I mean, God, I'd literally thrown myself at him and he still didn't want me. A man who'd probably slept with half the women on campus at school didn't... want... me.

"It's not what you think," he stated, breaking the silence and making me jump a little.

I looked over at him to see a small scowl on his face as he stared straight ahead, his jaw muscles pulsing in agitation.

"What is it then?" I asked softly, not knowing if he even heard me.

He turned the scowl on me then, narrowing his eyes as if he were sizing me up, maybe wondering if I could handle the truth or something. Then he shook his head a few times. "Nothing. I'll walk you to the door."

And that's exactly what he did, and after telling me he had a good time tonight and me thanking him once again, he brushed his lips against mine, waited for me to get inside the apartment then took off.

When I made it to bed, I lay there staring at the ceiling my brain on overload. Gable didn't want to sleep with me, but he wanted to sleep with his pen pal and I knew he *had* to know I was his pen pal. There'd been too many signs, too many coincidences for him not to know. But the rejection of tonight still hurt. What the hell was going on with him? I decided to dig a little, using my investigative skills (although to this point they'd been to use Tony to do all the investigating), and see if maybe I could get some answers. If not, Halloween was a week away and everything would be out in the open and I knew I'd get answers then.

And that scared the shit out of me.

Week Ten

Me: Hey, just wanted you to know I loved the tour Friday night. My treat next time. I'll look up something Seattle'ish to do that you don't know about ;) xo

Gable didn't reply.

He wasn't in class Monday nor was he at work the next two nights.

But he did reply to his fucking pen pal the next day.

From: 9565876 <student.9565876@hallervan.edu>

Subject: Halloween party

Date: October 28, 11:25 p.m.

To: 9543254 <student.9543254@hallervan.edu>

Hey,

Just wanted to let you know my roommate's going with me so I'll be there. Um, we're supposed to wear costumes, right?

Six

xo

From: 9543254 <student.9543254@hallervan.edu>

Subject: Halloween party

Date: October 28, 11:27 p.m.

To: 9565876 <student.9565876@hallervan.edu>

Six,

Can't wait to meet you. Costumes, yes. Masks, yes. You gonna be wearing what you described to me when you were in the SC sans the skirt and shirt? Fucking hope so.

xx

Seriously? This was really pissing me off that he was answering *her*, being nice to *her* and not me.

Holy Hayseuss Christo. I was jealous of my own fucking self. Unbelievable. And what was even more unbelievable was that as I sat there before replying, all I could think about was if I really could wear a bustier and all that went with it to the party without getting arrested.

Ugh. Stupid me. Also, stupid me and my big mouth for ever teasing him about wearing it. Dang. I'd have to ask Amy to see if it'd be too much.

From: 9565876 <student.9565876@hallervan.edu>

Subject: Bail money?

Date: October 28, 11:28 p.m.

To: 9543254 <student.9543254@hallervan.edu>

I'm assuming you'd bail me out when I got arrested for indecent exposure?

xo

From: 9543254 <student.9543254@hallervan.edu>

Subject: Au contraire

Date: October 28, 11:28 p.m.

To: 9565876 <student.9565876@hallervan.edu>

Six, if you were to wear that sexy as fuck outfit just for me, YOU'D have to bail ME out because I'd beat the shit out of anyone who looked at you.

xx

From: 9565876 <student.9565876@hallervan.edu>

Subject: Parlez-vous français?

Date: October 28, 11:29 p.m.

To: 9543254 <student.9543254@hallervan.edu>

Do you speak French??

xo

From: 9543254 <student.9543254@hallervan.edu>

Subject: Parlez whatever

Date: October 28, 11:30 p.m.

To: 9565876 <student.9565876@hallervan.edu>

Baby, I'll speak whatever language you want as long as I get to see you in that outfit...

xx

Wow. I shook my head because I was honestly hurt over his flirting with *me*. Yeah, ridiculous, I know.

Okay, if he could flirt with his pen pal while supposedly dating me, then so could I, so I decided to suck it up and just go for it. I mean, it *was* Halloween and I could probably get away with wearing the stupid outfit. And if things went bad, at least I'd look hot.

From: 9565876 <student.9565876@hallervan.edu>

Subject: No promises

Date: October 28, 3:50 p.m.

To: 9543254 <student.9543254@hallervan.edu>

I'll see what I can do

xo

~*~*~*~

"Black lace, huh?" Bodhi asked as he looked through various panties in a bin.

"Yep," I answered as I dug alongside him.

We were in Victoria's Secret in the mall the next day and I had to laugh at how casually he was searching for a pair of panties for my "costume."

"Perfect!" he yelled, holding up a pair of lacy hipster-type panties making several women in the store turn their heads to see him twirling them in the air with his finger.

I snatched them out of his hand. "Keep it down," I said, ducking my head and bugging my eyes out at him.

He looked around to see a few women still watching him. "It's okay! I'm gay!" he explained and the funny thing is, the ones looking at him raised their eyebrows, nodded, seeming to accept his explanation, and went on about their shopping. "Works every time," he mumbled with a snort. "Now for a bustier!" he all but yelled, and I was loath to shush him, possibly killing his excitement in the process, so all I could do was shake my head, rolling my eyes at the women who were now chuckling at us.

After shopping, we sat at a table in the food court eating Chinese that Bodhi bought since my checking account had taken a huge hit with my lingerie purchases.

"I like it. The robe is perfect to top it off." Bodhi said before sucking in a mouthful of lo mein noodles.

"You don't think it's too much? Too risqué?" I asked.

"It's risqué all right, but that's what makes it awesome! I especially like the stockings with the seam in the back." He shoved a small crab rangoon in his mouth.

"What if he's, like, in love with his pen pal then when I reveal it's me, he freaks because he's not in love with me *me* but her?"

"Then you deal with it. Are *you* in love with *him*?" Bodhi asked carefully, narrowing his eyes at me as I took a sip of egg drop soup from my spoon.

I shrugged a shoulder. "I don't know." And I didn't. I mean, how confusing was it that the guy I thought I might be in love with may be in love with my alter ego whom he might not know was me.

"But you said he's given you lots of hints that he knows it's you," he continued.

"I think he has but maybe it was just me hoping that he knew. God. When this semester's over, I'm getting a friggin' spa treatment and possibly hiring a shrink." I shook my head then took a bite of my spring roll.

"You'll be fine, Scout. And Amy and I have your back."

"Speaking of Amy, she said she's gonna dress in the Catwoman suit she wore a couple years ago. She said it's pretty sexy, so it'll make me not feel so naked."

"You know what? Fuck this. I know I told you I work that night, but I'm going with you. I'll ask Bob if I can come in an hour late. I've got a great Zorro costume, whip and all." He grinned.

I grinned back. It made me feel better that my friends would be with me in case things went to shit.

Before we left the mall, Bodhi and I stopped at a shoe store where I bought some sexy black stilettos then we hit the costume store where I bought a black, lacy Mardi Gras-type mask that came with a spray adhesive. It went perfectly with my outfit, and when I held it up to my face, Bodhi said if he didn't know it was me, he'd have no idea who it was. Awesome. Just what I needed in case I chickened out and didn't tell Gable who I really was.

We drove back to my apartment where we hung out for a bit, me putting everything on and giving Bodhi a fashion show.

"Damn, Scout. You're kinda making me rethink this whole gay thing," he muttered when I jerked my robe open at him like I was a flasher. "I think I'm poppin' a chubby."

I died laughing, falling on the bed with him where he'd been lying, head propped in his hand, elbow to the mattress, watching me model for him. I lifted my head and looked at him, wiggling my eyebrows. "It's never too late if you wanna go straight," I said, sitting up then opening my robe again showing him my bustier with a grin.

"God. You're beautiful," he answered, staring at me for a moment. Then he sat up. "But sorry. No chubby. I just have to pee." He jumped off my bed and left my room leaving me laughing in his wake.

I changed and we watched a little television then Bodhi had to leave for work. Before going, he bent and kissed my forehead telling me it would all work out in the end.

I smiled at him hoping he was right. Now if I could make it for two more days without having an anxiety attack, everything would be good.

~*~*~*~

I was probably making a mistake, but the next morning, I put my investigative skills to work and stopped Gable's brother, Lochlan, after biology class needing some answers as to why Gable was avoiding me.

"Hey, Lochlan, remember me?" I asked with a smile when I caught up to him on his way out of the building.

"Hey," he answered, stopping and smiling back. "Call me Loch. Yeah, you're Scout Patterson, Gable's girlfriend."

Well, that made me pull my head back in surprise.

"Uh, I wouldn't say I was his girlfriend..."

"Why? You're dating each other exclusively, right? I mean, I haven't seen him go out with anyone else in over a month and that's *huge* for him," he informed me with a chuckle.

Hm. Interesting.

"Do you have time to go get a coffee?" I inquired.

He looked at his watch. "Sure. My next class isn't for another hour."

"Great. Do you want to just go to the student center then?"

He nodded and we took off walking to the center that was nearby. He insisted on buying my latte and we sat down at my usual table.

"So what's up?" he asked, taking a sip of his drink.

I was nervous, not sure if this was cool of me to do, but I had to get some information before going into the party tomorrow night blind.

"Well, this is kinda weird, but I had a few questions about Gable." I bit my lip wondering if he'd tell me to fuck off.

"Okay. Nothing sexual, I hope, 'cause that'd be pretty gross."

I laughed. "No, nothing like that. I, uh, was just wondering about him. You see, we, um, started getting close a couple times." I saw his face scrunch up as if he thought I meant sexually. "No!" I said with another laugh. "I don't mean sex-wise!"

"Thank God," he mumbled. He ran his hand through his hair which made me shake my head because his mannerisms were so like his brother's.

"I mean, just close, you know? But each time, he's pulled away for a while. Do you have any idea why?"

"Not really my story to tell…"

I bit my lips and raised my eyebrows at him. Aha. There *was* something to Gable's aloofness.

He frowned. "But I think you deserve to know because I know how secretive he is on top of being a broody bastard." His eyes had a hint of humor in them before he took another drink then looked around as if he was making sure Gable wasn't anywhere near. "Gable had a girlfriend, Mia, who he met in high school. They started dating when they were seniors. Dated at the beginning of their freshman year in college too. She went to UDub, though."

I nodded, looking around now too, a little paranoid that Gable might catch us talking about him.

Loch sighed. "Things were always up and down with them. They were pretty intense, you know, fought a lot, young love and all, I guess. I mean, he'd get a new tattoo and she'd get mad. She was pretty preppy and I guess she didn't like it that her boyfriend wasn't. I honestly didn't know why they went out in the first place. Anyway, he got tired of it all and finally broke things off. A week later, she died in a car wreck."

I sucked in a breath at hearing that, knowing exactly where he was going with it.

"Gable of course felt horrible. Seemed like it took him forever to get over it, the guilt and all."

"Yeah," I whispered, my eyes tearing up as I stared into my cup.

"He also lost his best friend that night."

My head shot up at hearing this. Oh, God, no. Poor Gable.

Loch nodded then sighed again. "Riley Cooper. He and Gable had been best friends since, like, seventh grade. Coop was driving, it was raining, they think he swerved to avoid an animal or something, he overcorrected and the car rolled at least three times. Killed both of them."

Ah. Coop. I'd seen an "RIP Coop" tattoo over Gable's heart when I'd caught him at work with his shirt off. But wait. Both? I frowned at Loch.

He looked at me grimly pursing his lips together. "They were together, Mia and Coop. They'd been seeing each other behind Gable's back for a while. He didn't find that out until a month after they died then it all hit him hard." Loch leaned back in his chair and took in a deep breath letting it out slowly. "Makes sense, though. Riley was more her type, clean-cut, studying to be a lawyer. He went to UDub too, so I guess it was convenient for them." He shrugged.

"God," I whispered. Oh, Gable. When I'd written to him about Hayden and Ivy cheating behind my back, he'd known exactly what I'd been talking about since he'd lost his girlfriend and best friend all at once too. Oh, God.

"Yeah. He was pretty torn up." He stretched out more in his chair and looked at me and it was uncanny how much he looked like his brother, but I noticed that his eyes were a little darker than Gable's. "So that's why I said that his only seeing you is a big deal. He hasn't dated anyone seriously since they died. I mean, his bedroom has had a revolving door on it for a while. My brothers and I used to make bets on what hair color would come out of his room each morning."

My eyebrows came together. "Hair color?"

"You know, the girls and whether they'd be blond, red, brunette. Long, short. I made fifty bucks one week."

Dear God.

He chuckled at the look I must've had on my face. "He's calmed down a lot this year, though."

This year? Dear God!

"But he seems to really be into you. Talked about you some. Zeke, Ryker and I were hoping he's finally settling down some."

"He talks about me?" I asked. "What does he say?"

"I don't know, just things like you went to a movie and on the ghost tour." He shrugged a shoulder then sat up in his chair putting his elbows on the table and clasping his hands together. "But I'm telling you, that's huge for him." He looked at his watch. "Hey, I need to get to class. Look, don't tell him we talked. He'd kick my ass if he knew." He stood and so did I.

"Thank you, Loch. I really appreciate it. I won't say a word," I promised. He smiled then left me standing there kind of in shock. "He talks about me," I mumbled as I walked toward the door.

According to Loch, that was a big deal. Huge. And it made me feel good that Gable did care for me, that maybe I wasn't the pathetic doormat for him that I'd felt like at times. But, God, he'd been through so much pain. My heart ached for him as I walked across campus heading to my car, knowing that the reason he probably didn't want to get close to me was because he didn't want to get hurt again.

And I knew I'd have to make sure that didn't happen.

~*~*~*~

Oh, but Mr. Gable Powers was in fine form that night at work.

On this awesome Wednesday evening, the night before the party, he was back to his old assholish ways when all I wanted to do was give him a big hug for all he'd gone through with his girlfriend and best friend. Wonderful.

I brought my first order to him and saw he was leaning on his forearms on the counter seemingly flirting with a redhead who wore an emerald green dress that showed lots of cleavage and hit her at mid-thigh as she sat at the bar with her legs crossed. She had on four-inch expensive looking emerald green suede stilettos and she looked to be in her forties. Don't get me wrong, she was gorgeous and all—big boobs, shapely legs— but what the fuck? When I walked up, Gable popped a cherry in his mouth as he pushed off a forearm and stood, grinned at her, a little too suggestively for my taste I might add, then looked at me with a smirk and said, "What can I do you for, Scout?" Then he chuckled at his comment and winked at me.

Asshole.

I handed him my order ticket, trying hard to keep the hurt off my face, but I'm not sure if I succeeded. I was hurt because he hadn't talked to me since last Friday when he'd given me a spectacular orgasm, hurt because he hadn't wanted to stay the night with me, hurt because he hadn't bothered to answer my text I'd sent on Sunday, but, hurt worse because, by God, he'd taken the time to talk to his pen pal who was really the real me but not. Oh, hell, you know what I mean. Shit.

And now I was hurt because he was talking to this woman.

"Scout?" the redhead said glancing over at me. "That's an unusual name." Then she smiled at me.

Great. She was nice. Couldn't be a bitch so I could be one right back to her. Of course not. So I gave her a small smile in return then turned my back to her so she wouldn't engage me anymore because I was afraid I'd say something rude.

When Gable had filled my tray with my order, he flashed his lopsided grin at me, winked again and as I picked up the tray, the woman spoke to him. "Okay, so you were telling me about the corbelled arch on your grandparents' courtyard. Are you sure it's not bonded? What kind of stone is in the voussoir?"

And she was smart and into architecture so they had something in common. Great again.

I walked away going to different tables to fill their orders, the whole time trying to reign in my jealousy at the fact that he could go five days without talking to me but could chat away with some gorgeous random woman at the bar.

And that pissed me off but good.

But I guessed he didn't owe me anything because what even the hell were we? We weren't boyfriend and girlfriend (or does climaxing on a guy's hand automatically make it so?). I huffed out a frustrated laugh at that making my patrons look at me strangely. Whatever.

As I continued setting drinks down, I wondered if Gable was seeing other women. Loch said he wasn't but how did he know for sure. I mean, we hadn't said we were exclusive so he could've been seeing them just not bringing them home for his brothers to witness.

And the last thing I thought about as I took orders from a family of five was that if Gable didn't know I was his pen pal, then he kind of *was* cheating on me since he wanted to meet *her,* who was really me but not, *and* he said he wanted to fuck her but he obviously didn't want to fuck me.

Oh.

My.

God.

Forget about the spa treatment. I was all in for seeing a shrink then checking into a padded room when the semester was over.

 So the rest of the night stunk to high heaven because Red stayed at the bar the entire time chatting Gable up, and every time I had an order filled, he and I didn't have a chance to talk (which was probably good because it wouldn't have been pretty on my part anyway), but he *would* give me sexy looks and wink at me. What did that mean?

Thirty minutes before my shift was over, I decided I was done, so over everything. I figured I'd still go to the party tomorrow night, reveal myself to Gable, have a few drinks with Amy and Bodhi then get the hell out of there, writing Gable off as a loss. Yep. I'd just go back to my original plan which was not getting involved with him in the first place. Sounded good.

Ten minutes before my shift was over, I saw Red get up to leave and watched as Gable walked her out, and forgetting my awesome plan of writing him off, I felt my head explode at seeing him go with her. I looked around for Natalie but had to wait until she finished taking orders at a table then I walked with her to the kitchen and said, "Watch my section, please. I'll be right back."

"Everything okay?" she asked.

"We'll see," I muttered as I semi-stomped through the place toward the front door.

When I got outside, I looked around and didn't see anyone. There were no cars leaving and I wasn't sure if Red could've left that quickly, so I walked through the parking lot like a damned creeper, checking every car to see if they were inside any of them doing God knew what. When I found that every car was empty, even his (which I just *knew* would have the windows fogged over because she'd be straddling his lap while he gave *her* a spectacular orgasm but it didn't), a thought hit me. And then my heart was in my damned throat as I jogged to the back knowing I'd see him have Red pressed against the back of the bar kissing her and telling her that she tasted good. And that made me furious.

I rounded the corner, fists clenched, ready to chew some serious ass then break up with him, even if we weren't officially together and I know you can't break up with someone you were never with but what the fuck ever, that was my plan, but that's when I saw him standing at the steps smoking a cigarette. And Red was nowhere to be seen.

I came up short, my heart in my throat thunking back to its original spot in my chest as I watched him take a drag and blow out the smoke. And feeling like an ass for thinking the worst in him, I quietly turned to go back the way I'd come and sneak back inside without his seeing me, but my stealth was all for naught.

"What's up, Priss?" he questioned making me stop.

Shit.

I turned around knowing I'd been caught and walked toward him slowly trying to think of a lie.

"Uh, I was just checking to make sure the, uh, the, uh, Dumpster wasn't full." Yeah, that sounded good.

"And you went out the front instead of the back?" he asked, taking another drag before blowing the smoke out of his nose. How he made that look sexy, I have no idea, but he damned sure did.

God, I was seriously screwed with this man.

"Um, Glen's mopping and I didn't want to walk across the wet floor," I answered lamely.

"Uh huh." He flicked the butt to the side and walked toward me, stalked really, as if I were his prey, his eyes shining and intense on mine. Gah. "I think you might've been jealous that I was talking to Dr. Miller and you thought you'd catch me back here with her."

Dr. Miller? Oh, man, she was probably a professor from one of his architect classes. Shit. Shit!

As I watched him approach, I gave an almost imperceptible shake of my head in answer to his question then tried hard to appear as innocent as I could, hoping that was a tad bit of amusement I saw in his eyes as he stared me down. When he reached me, he just kept walking making me back up until I hit the wall then he put both hands to either side of my head and bent down to get in my face. "I think that's exactly what you thought."

Now I couldn't look him in the eye as I chewed on the inside of my lip, too embarrassed that he'd seen right through me.

"Am I right?" he asked, his eyes narrowed and piercing mine when I made the mistake of looking back at him, and I saw that all amusement was now replaced with not a small amount of pissed off.

Yikes.

At his question, I bit my lips and nodded, doing this not enthusiastically, mind you.

He shoved off the wall with his hands. "That's what I thought," he mumbled then turned to go back inside.

Wait. What?

I took a step after him and asked, "Well, what was I supposed to think?"

He turned and stared at me for a moment then said, "I'm with you, Scout," as if that explained everything.

I huffed at that, frowning at him. What the heck did that mean? So I asked him. "What does that mean?"

The muscles in his jaws were jumping as he kept looking at me. "It means I'm *with* you, Scout."

"You're with me…" I mumbled, looking down at my sneakers, shaking my head in confusion.

"Yeah."

I looked back up at him. "I don't know what that means, Gable."

Then he moved so fast I could only gasp as he pushed me against the wall again, his body pressing hard into mine, his hand wrapping in the back of my hair and tilting my head to the side as his mouth came slamming down on mine.

Whoa.

He kissed me hard as if proving a point and when he pulled away, I was left standing there breathing hard looking up at him as he scowled down at me.

"Get it now?" he spat.

Uh, no. I didn't. And why was he so angry? God, why was everything so confusing when it came to him?

I shook my head and it seemed to exasperate him.

"No?" he asked, all out of patience, hands on hips looking at me in disbelief.

I shook my head again as I bit my lip, not knowing what was going on here.

It was his turn to shake his head as he stepped back into me. "I'm *with* you," he muttered that puzzling decree again, then took my chin in his fingers and leaned down touching his lips to mine softly as if to make up for the punishing kiss he'd just given me. He pulled away to look at me, his honey eyes smoldering into mine, then mine dropped to his chest where my hands rested. The next thing I knew, he lifted my chin again coming back in for another kiss, and I guess he was finished being gentle because this kiss went off-the-charts scorching hot in about one-point-two seconds as our tongues twirled together which made my stomach flutter like crazy.

His hands were everywhere on me then, one sliding beneath my short jersey where it stopped just under the swell of my breast and his thumb began sliding over my nipple making me shiver. His other hand slid down to cup my butt, jerking me hard into his hips as he groaned into my mouth.

I too got caught up in the kiss, my leg curling around the back of one of his, my hands going up to where my fingers threaded into his hair, tugging, holding him tighter to me. I was so lost to him, so lost *in* him, that when he suddenly tore his lips from mine, pulling back to look intensely down at me, and the expression I saw was one of almost anguish covering his face, I was completely baffled.

Uh. What in the world was going on in his head? One minute he's telling me he's with me, whatever he meant by that, and the next he's looking at me as if I was the biggest mistake he's ever made. God.

His demeanor jarred my fogged brain into action and I remembered then that we needed to talk. I also remembered the reason I was out here in the first place which was to possibly catch him making out with his professor. Crap.

I extracted myself from his arms, dropping my hands (and foot) and stepping to the side to put some space between us, the whole time trying to even out my breathing. I swear, the man was the embodiment of sex itself, making me want him any time he touched me which was just unnerving. When I got myself together somewhat, I glanced up to see the pained look still on his face as if he regretted what had just happened between us.

"What?" I whispered with a frown.

He closed his eyes for several seconds then opened them before taking a deep breath. "It's complicated."

"Yeah," I answered. His head came up and his eyes held mine, regarding me as if he was afraid that I knew about his past, which I, of course, did, but he didn't know that. "I don't know what's going on, Gable. You haven't talked to me in five days. And then you tell me you're with me but don't explain it. I'm not sure I understand."

He backed away and went to the steps to pick up his pack of cigarettes, getting one out and lighting it. I watched as he sucked in deep then blew out the smoke.

"I'm fucked up, Scout. Screwed up," he answered, his eyes cutting through me as he took another drag. "You were smart, you'd leave me the fuck alone." He then looked away as he took another hit from his cigarette.

Ugh. Same thing Hayden had said to me which had been a big fucking excuse. And now I was pissed.

"You know what? I hate when guys do shit like this," I hissed, throwing my arms up. Gable's head came up and his eyes pierced mine as I continued. "Suck you into their lives then feed you that bullshit line. That's a fucking copout, Gable, and you know it." I glared at him, angry that he'd gone to that.

He narrowed his eyes. "Oh, yeah? Had this happen before, have you? What, your ex cheat with your best friend? Then tell you he's fucked up? That what happened?"

I now scowled at him. We'd only talked about this through email, never in person, so now I was sure he knew we were pen pals. "Yeah. Had exactly that happen," I snapped.

He didn't even flinch. Yep. Definitely knew. He took one last drag on his cigarette before flicking it away. Then after exhaling the smoke, he gazed at me for a moment then took a deep breath in through his nose, blew it back out and took a step toward me. We were still about three feet apart at that point but the distance felt like miles. His eyes scanned my face and my hair as if he was trying to memorize what I looked like then they came back to mine. "So fuckin' beautiful. So fuckin' hard to resist," he mumbled as he shook his head. I started to tell him not to resist but he spoke before I could. "But I've got shit goin' on and I can't do this right now."

It took me a moment to process that and when I did, my brows came down. Okay, even though I knew we weren't technically together, was he saying he was breaking up with me? But he'd just told me he was with me! God! He was so frustrating!

"Ar—are you telling me we're over?" I asked, my mouth instantly dry and tears stinging the backs of my eyes.

"Not fair for me to ask you to wait until I get shit sorted, so, yeah, I guess I am." His eyes, void of any emotion at all, held mine.

Oh, my God. Was he kidding me right now?

Wow. Just fucking wow.

I opened my mouth to respond then closed it. I opened it once again and closed it again. Well, three times a charm and all that, so I once again opened it, but still having no clue what I'd say if I could've actually spoken, closed it one last time. Then keeping my eyes fixed to his and seeing that he wasn't budging on what he'd said, I nodded a couple times, still reeling from what had just happened, and unable to hold the tears back, stood humiliated in front of him as they spilled down my cheeks.

Then I walked away.

~*~*~*~

The next part was carried out in a zombified state:

I went inside the bar, found Jack, told him I didn't feel well and needed to leave. When I got his okay, I clocked out, walked outside, got in my car and drove home.

At my apartment, I went inside, went to my bedroom, got a change of clothes, went to the bathroom, took a shower, dressed, brushed my teeth, went to my bedroom, got in bed and fell asleep.

When I awoke the next morning, I knew I'd been on some serious autopilot the night before because I was puzzled at how I'd gotten into bed much less gotten home.

Weird.

After lying there staring at the ceiling for a while, I got up and went to the kitchen to get breakfast seeing Amy sitting at the table in her usual "I hate morning" position as she ate her cereal. I walked to the counter, grabbed the bag of bagels, got one out, pulled a knife out of the drawer to cut it in two, put the other half back in the bag, twisted the bag shut then dropped the other half into the toaster.

Jeez. I was still in zombie mode.

"You okay?" Amy mumbled as I pushed the button down on the toaster.

I turned and leaned my butt against the counter. "Yeah. Why?"

She looked at me through narrowed eyes. "You're still moving like a robot. I said hi to you last night when you came in but you acted like you didn't hear me or even know I was there, and, like WALL-E or some shit, you did your nightly routine then went to bed without even acknowledging me. So, again, you okay?"

My eyes dropped to the floor and what had happened between Gable and me finally hit. My eyes teared up and I looked up at her. "No, I don't think I am."

"Oh, sweetie, what's wrong?" she asked, pushing away from the table and standing coming over to me.

I looked at her as a tear made its way down my cheek. "Gable said we're over." And that's when it really hit me and I hiccupped out a sob as the tears came one after the other.

"Oh, honey, I'm sorry," Amy whispered and took me in her arms, letting me cry on her shoulder.

There was a knock at the door then I heard a key in the knob and Bodhi made his way inside.

"Just got off work and I'm starv—" he started then I heard him ask, "What's going on?"

I pulled my head away from Amy and looked up at him not able to contain the choked sob that came out and then he was there, taking me into his arms and letting me cry against his chest. He rubbed his hand over my back several times whispering sweet things to me as I clutched his t-shirt with my fists.

When I was cried out, I brought my head back to look up at him and I knew from the look on his face that Amy had communicated to him somehow what had happened.

"It's gonna be okay, Scout. Promise," he said looking down at me with a small smile.

I nodded as another tear slipped out. Amy handed me a napkin and I used it to wipe my eyes then nose.

"I—I feel like an idiot," I told them. "I knew he'd hurt me."

Bodhi ushered me over to sit in a chair at the table and Amy brought me a freshly toasted bagel that she'd put grape jelly on, placing the plate and a glass of orange juice in front of me.

"Thank you," I mumbled, staring at my breakfast knowing I'd lost my appetite.

They both sat down at the table with me.

"What happened?" Bodhi asked, eating what I was pretty sure was the first bagel I'd put in to toast.

I sighed then told them what'd happened and afterward we sat in silence for a few minutes.

"He didn't break up with you," Bodhi finally said making my head jerk up to look at him.

"What?" I asked.

"I mean, he told you he had to work through some things, right?"

I nodded.

"He didn't break up with you," he repeated.

"So when he said we're over he was just kidding," I said sarcastically.

"His brother told you about what had happened to him," Amy reminded me. "So I think Bodhi's right. I mean, he may have said you're over, but I don't think he meant it. From what you've told us, pretty sure he's totally into you."

"What?" I asked incredulously. "May I remind you that he fucking broke things off!"

"Yeah, but I don't think he meant to," Bodhi threw out there.

"You guys are delusional," I mumbled.

"You're still going to the party tonight," Amy stated. "You can confront him there."

Oh, shit! The party. Oh, hell no.

"No! I can't go!" I dropped my head into my hand with a groan.

"Oh, you're going, all right," Bodhi said. "And you're gonna knock him dead with how hot you look. He'll change his tune after that."

I shook my head. No way was I going. No way.

"We'll be right there with you, Scout. It's all gonna work out," Amy added.

Sure it would. I'd find him at the party, tell him I was his pen pal, he'd tell me he hated liars, and even though my dear friends were trying to convince me that Gable and I weren't over, when I told him, we'd be *really* over and that'd be the end of that.

Sounded like loads of fun.

I couldn't wait.

Week Ten—Party night

From: 9543254 <student.9543254@hallervan.edu>

Subject: Tonight

Date: October 31, 9:02 a.m.

To: 9565876 student.9565876@hallervan.edu

Six,

Can't wait to see you tonight. I'll be the one dressed as Arrow in all black, hooded jacket and jeans with a bow and quiver and a mask, of course. I'll be there around 9. Don't know if you've been in the Sig Eps' house before, but when you walk in, go to your left. I'll be waiting in the hallway by the kitchen bar.

See you soon.

xx

My stomach flipped when I read Gable's email that morning. If Amy hadn't been right there when my phone dinged, I would've written back and told him I wasn't coming. But she was and she grabbed my phone and answered for me.

From: 9565876 <student.9565876@hallervan.edu>

Subject: Tonight

Date: October 31, 9:04 a.m.

To: 9543254 <student.9543254@hallervan.edu>

I'll be there.

And that was that.

~*~*~*~

I went to my classes that morning, thanking God that I didn't run into Gable and now here I was getting ready for the stupid party that neither Bodhi nor Amy would let me get out of. The good thing was, they'd plied me with alcohol so I wasn't nearly as nervous as I thought I'd be.

When Amy and I walked into the living room, Bodhi let out a loud wolf whistle then exclaimed, "Damn! You'll be the hottest chicks there!"

I had to admit, we did look good. Amy had on her Catwoman outfit that was skintight, and she looked sexy as hell. I had on my lingerie along with the four-inch black stilettos I'd bought and the robe covering it all. I'd poufed my hair big with lots of big curls and done my makeup dramatic, giving myself smoky cat eyes with eyeliner even though they'd be mostly covered with my mask. I'd borrowed Amy's scarlet lipstick so we matched and that topped off my outfit. Then we'd sprayed the adhesive to my mask and pressed it to my face and I was ready.

"Not looking so bad yourself," Amy replied.

Bodhi's Zorro costume did look good on him.

"If I didn't know any better, I'd think Antonio Banderas was in my living room right now," I stated with a giggle, the vodka I'd been drinking having loosened me up quite a bit.

"Okay, enough with the booze," Amy said, taking the glass out of my hands. "Ready?" she asked, looking closely at me.

I sighed. "As I'll ever be."

"Let's go over the game plan again," Bodhi repeated for the fiftieth time.

"I think we've got it down," I griped. "We go in, we get a drink, I find Gable, I tell him who I am, if I need your help, I wave at you and you come over and get me the hell out of there. Do I have it right?" I raised an eyebrow at Bodhi.

"You do. All right. Let's do this," he muttered and we left the apartment, piled into Amy's Mazda SUV and headed to the party.

~*~*~*~

I don't know if I'd ever been brave before, but as we walked inside the frat house, I felt like a goddamned hero for even showing up.

I know that sounds stupid, but that shit was scary. Even though I was a bit tipsy (I'd snuck the fifth of vodka with me in my robe pocket and had a few hits on the way over from where I sat alone in the backseat) I could still feel my heart in my throat.

But I was so glad my friends were with me because without them, I think this bravery gig I had going on would've backfired the minute I got out of the vehicle. As it was, being sandwiched between Amy, who led the way, and Bodhi who was at my back, I was doing pretty well.

"Drink," Amy directed once we were inside, having to yell this over the loudly thumping music that was playing, and I followed her through the crowd to a corner where several guys were manning a keg.

Since beer had made my shit list when I'd gotten drunk several weeks ago, I bypassed the cup that was offered me and pulled out the vodka bottle instead.

"Are you shitting me?" Amy snapped when she saw it and tried grabbing it from me.

"Just one more," I explained, then took a huge gulp and gladly handed her what remained.

"Don't get sloppy," she responded but I could see she sympathized with me.

"There he is," Bodhi said, his tall frame making him head and shoulders above everyone else and helping him see over the crowd. I looked up at him and he nodded toward his left. I know he saw the fear in my eyes because he grabbed my hand and squeezed it. "You'll be fine."

"You will," Amy agreed with a nod then put her hand to the middle of my back and gave me a small push in the direction Bodhi had been looking.

When I turned and looked at both of them, Amy smiled with a nod and Bodhi gave me a thumbs up, then I continued on my way to where I knew Gable would be.

I pushed my way through the crowd catching several guys giving me appreciative leers, and one even stopped me to ask for my number, which oddly gave me the confidence to stay the course and talk to Gable. I won't mention the guy who tried to feel me up in between the confidence-building I was receiving, but anyway, as I made my way over, I saw through the throng of partygoers Gable standing where he said he would be, talking to two girls who were dressed like Playboy Bunnies. One was rubbing herself all over him and I noticed that he wasn't denying her the contact. Jerk. And this gave me even more confidence to confront him because I'd had enough of his shit. He was a cheater and a jerk and a bastard and I was done with him. This may have been the alcohol talking, but at that point in time, I was finished with his hotter than hot assholish self. It may have helped too when I turned and tiptoed up to see Bodhi watching me from across the room giving me a nod.

I stood at the fringe of the revelers waiting for Gable to finish talking with the Playmates and was somewhat impressed with his costume. He had on a black, leather jacket that was tight enough that anyone could see that he was buff underneath it, the black hood on his head making him look a little sinister and the mask he wore doing a good job of disguising his identity. He wore black jeans and black military-style boots and of course, the bow and a quiver strapped on his back. I hated to admit it, but he looked extremely sexy and I felt my confidence waiver a bit. Just as I was about to turn around and go back to Bodhi and Amy, I was bumped into by a very good looking guy (from what I could tell since he was wearing a mask) who was dressed as a fireman and who immediately wrapped his arm around my waist pulling me into his front, and apologizing for running into me. He had gorgeous white teeth as he smiled down at me and I was just about to ask his name when I felt someone grab my hand and yank me away not only from him but from the slew of celebrants that surrounded me.

"Six. It's you," Gable muttered as he still held my hand but looked me over from head to toe. "Fuck... me..." he mumbled.

"In the flesh," I replied, now feeling fairly bold at his reaction but also disappointed that he didn't know it was me. But the vodka swimming in my veins didn't let me feel that way for long. No, it emboldened me and I was glad. So I'd play along for a bit before spoiling it all for him. Whatever.

He stared at me for a moment before he spoke again. "May I?" he asked and I frowned not sure what he wanted. When his hand tugged on the belt of my robe, I knew he wanted to see what I wore, and what the hell, I knew I looked good, so I nodded.

I looked down to watch him untie my sash and saw his hand shaking a bit. Hm. He was nervous. Good. And that made me feel even more fearless, as if I had all the power here which was awesome.

When he got my belt undone, he put his hands inside my robe, opening it with the backs as he pushed them out to each side.

"Holy fuck," he muttered as he saw what I was wearing. "Jesus Christ, Six. You're fucking stunning."

I smirked at him knowing he'd never get to experience all the stunning that came with me, which was a weird thought, but hello, vodka.

Then his hands slid all the way inside to the back of my waist and he pulled me into him hard, surprising the hell out of me.

"Wanna fuck you, Six. Damn. I think I might be in love with you," he whispered into my ear.

And, oh, God, I wanted that so badly, wanted him to want me, wanted him to be in love with me that all my senses went on the blink and I whispered back, "Then have me."

He stepped back and looked down at me, his whiskey eyes behind his mask penetrating mine making me suck in a breath at the lust I saw there. Dang.

"Come with me," he said, taking my hand and pulling me down the hallway into a darkened room, closing the door behind us. Then he was there, right there, his mouth crashing down on mine, his hands inside my robe, one gliding around my waist where he held fast, the other sliding up the front of my bustier to cup my breast.

And I loved it. Loved every bit of it.

My hands went up and pushed his hood down then my fingers folded into the hair at the back of his head, tugging, pulling, wrenching him tighter to me making him groan into my mouth. Then I lost his mouth as he moved it along my jaw, to my neck where he nipped at me, making me shiver against him. His hands then moved up to my shoulders pushing my robe down them and off where it fluttered to the floor.

I couldn't see his face, only his outline from where he stood, but I knew he'd taken off his mask. He then unzipped his jacket and tossed it on the floor behind him and then I had him back, his mouth covering mine again, his tongue finding mine, twisting with it and making me moan. God, he felt so good pressed against me, his body so hard everywhere and I found myself pulling at the t-shirt he wore, tugging it out of his jeans then pulling it and his hoodie up over his head and off. My lips went to his chest, licking over what I knew were numerous tattoos that I wished I could see and ask him about, but it was too dark, of course, and what was now happening between us was too frantic, too hot and I was going to take all I could in that moment. A guttural sound escaped his mouth when my hand dropped down to brush over his chiseled abs at the same time my tongue grazed over his nipple. Then he'd had enough of my perusal of his body and was back in control, his mouth and hands back on me, seeking to give me as much pleasure as they could. He kissed the swell of my breasts as one hand slid to the back to cup my butt, the other running down my belly to between my legs where he curled his fingers over me making me squirm against him, my stomach flip flopping at the same time.

"Already fucking wet for me," he said hoarsely as he slipped a finger under my panties to move slowly through the slickness. When his finger entered me, I dug mine into his shoulders and my head went back against the door as I gasped.

"Oh, God," I breathed out, feeling my insides tightening as I headed toward a climax, his finger continuing to move inside, his thumb circling, bringing me closer.

Then his hand was gone making me whimper in protest, but then he picked me up, carrying me to the bed and setting me down on it where he knelt in front of me, removing my shoes then ran his hands up my legs over my stockings and to my waist to draw my panties down my legs slowly.

"You're perfect," he rasped as he stood, watching me as he unbuttoned his jeans then pushing them and his boxer briefs down and off before climbing onto the bed and pinning me beneath him so that he was cradled against my body between my legs, his weight on his forearms as he gazed down at me. I felt him hard against my pelvis and my hips tilted up involuntarily causing us both to hiss at the friction it created.

There was a small amount of light coming in through the blinds of the window, so I could see his face a bit although most of it was in shadows, but on it I saw an expression of pure desire as if he craved me, longed for me, his eyes burning into mine.

Oh, my God.

Then his lips came down to kiss me, and it was so sweet, so soft that I wanted to cry.

"Make love to me, please," I begged shamelessly against his lips, so ready for him, tired of having waited so long for this, wanting him inside me now. *Now.*

He reached for his jeans to get a condom and I heard it tear then he was resting between my legs again looking down at me with hunger in his eyes.

"Been wanting this for so long," he whispered, echoing my thoughts exactly, then he slid inside me smoothly. The moment he filled me I grasped his biceps, then cried out, coming instantly. "Baby," he groaned as he started moving, filling me so fully each time he entered me making my neck arch as I gasped at how good he felt.

He moved in and out of me slowly, thrusting in languidly, his eyes holding mine the whole time. "You feel so fucking good, baby. Been dreaming of this every night," he said huskily, his head dipping down to brush my lips with his as his hips rolled into mine over and over again.

He moved his hands under my bottom and tilted my hips to his as he increased his pace, going deeper with each thrust, making my breath catch each time he buried himself inside. Oh, my.

"So tight, ah, fuck," he mumbled as he continued pumping inside me, burying himself to the root on each drive forward.

And, God, this was perfect. It was everything I'd dreamed it'd be. And I loved him. God help me, but I loved him.

His hands moved from under me then found mine, and lacing his fingers with mine, he pulled my arms over my head where he pressed my hands into the pillow as the weight of his body covered me as he continued sliding in and out of me, making my back arch each time he moved inside.

"Fucking love this..." he whispered, his breath hot at my ear. "Wanted you forever."

"Oh, God," I gasped as, holy shit, I felt another climax building, and it was going to be big.

"I feel you, baby," he mumbled, his mouth pressed to my ear. "Let it go, Priss."

"Oh... my... God..." I breathed out. "Ohmigod, ohmigod, ohmigod!" And I was there. And it *was* big. *My entire body locking up as the waves of my orgasm shot through me in white hot bolts of heat that seared my veins making my toes curl*, big. *Feet pushing off the bed, body arching up as I cried out*, big. Holy fricking frick.

When I floated back inside myself, it was then I realized Gable had called me Priss. He *did* know it was me. Oh, thank God. Tears of relief rolled down the sides of my face, and I was so elated that it was me he wanted, me he'd dreamed about, that the beauty of it made me gasp out a sob of sheer happiness. It felt like the weight of the world had been lifted from my shoulders.

I buried my face in his neck and murmured, "Gable," kissing him softly there and felt him tense against me and he stilled his movements. But after a beat, he pulled his head back and looked down at me, his face still covered in shadow so I couldn't see his expression, but I just knew it had to be filled with warmth because I sensed it, literally felt in my bones and I knew that this was where we'd been headed the entire time. There was nothing between us now. No secrets. No lies. We were where we were supposed to be.

And it was heaven.

He leaned down and touched his mouth to mine then started moving inside me again, slow and easy, watching me, the delicious friction of his thrusts stirring my body again, the sensation growing with each roll of his hips. As he raced toward his own release, he started pumping more powerfully, faster, his hands clasping mine hard, pressing them deeper into the pillow, his body gliding against mine urgently, building the tension inside me until I cried out with my climax.

His wasn't far behind as he surged forward with several jarring thrusts before groaning out a curse with his release then his body dropped, covering mine as I trembled beneath him.

Oh… my.

We both lay there breathing heavily, the rhythm of our breaths almost in time with the music blasting from outside the door. He let my hands go and rose up on his forearms, bringing his head up and I could see him smiling down at me, his face bathed in the glow of the streetlight outside the window then his lips were on mine, administering a mind-shattering kiss.

"Be back," he whispered, then got off the bed, a shadow walking toward the adjoining bathroom. When he came back, he lay down next to me, pulling the comforter over us then wrapping his arms around me pulled my back to his front tightly, kissing my neck a few times before his head dropped and I heard his breathing even out.

Wow. I was in bed with Gable Powers who I'd just had sex with and who was now holding me in his arms. The me he knew was his pen pal. The me he'd wanted all along. And with a smile on my face, I too drifted off.

~*~*~*~

I lay with my face turned to the side on the bed, my arms splayed out to my sides, hands clutching the sheet, on my knees with my ass in the air as Gable held my hips and pounded me from behind. And it was amazing.

I wasn't sure how long it'd been since we'd fallen asleep, maybe an hour, but the next thing I knew, I'd been awakened by Gable's lips between my legs. And, my God, he knew exactly what to do with those lips.

"Oh, shit," I'd whispered as he dragged his tongue over my folds then thrust it inside me as he sucked, licked, kissed. My hands were wrapped in his hair holding him to me as I unabashedly tilted my hips up and I felt him grin against me.

"Like me eating your pussy," he mumbled.

I didn't think he wanted an answer so I didn't give him one which was fine because I was too busy panting, loving what he was doing to me. I then felt his finger inside me and when he moved up and sucked my clitoris into his hot, wet mouth, that was all it took for me to unravel right there in front of him, for him.

Good lord.

He'd pulled back and flipped me around to my stomach and that's where we were now, him drilling inside me from behind, going so deep that I was making incoherent noises at each thrust, little mews of pleasure.

He leaned over me, his hand going to one of my breasts, rolling my nipple between his thumb and finger and I felt the quickening inside me again.

"Oh, my God," I whispered breathily when his hand moved down between my legs priming me for yet another orgasm.

"Want you to come for me again," he muttered in my ear as he drove into me repeatedly and I didn't disappoint as I exploded around him, my hands gripping the sheet hard, my head coming up off the bed as I screamed out my release.

Holy shit.

Then his thrusts became more forceful, shallower and I felt him go rigid against me as he came, his arm around me clutching me tightly, his breath on my back hot and fast. He fell to the side to his back pulling me with him and I lay with my head on his outstretched arm as we both breathed heavily.

"Jesus. That was beautiful, Six," he said after a minute. His head turned toward mine, but it was still so dark, I could only see an outline of his face. Then he leaned in and brushed my lips with his then dislodged his arm from underneath me and got out of bed.

And that's when my heart seized. Six? Why was he calling me Six again? I frowned as I lay staring at the darkened ceiling. He knew it was me. He *knew* it. He'd called me Priss. *He knew*. So why was he pretending he didn't?

And, oh, God, I wanted to scream at him for that. I wanted to tell him I'd made a huge mistake, a mammoth mistake by being with him. I wanted to tell him that he was a coward, that he was a craven prick who didn't deserve me.

"It's Scout," I whispered, but he was already heading toward the adjoining bathroom to discard the condom.

Then the thought hit me that maybe he didn't know it was me and that maybe he'd only been thinking of me as he fucked his pen pal, and had called "her" the wrong name.

And that thought was even more distressing.

I saw his shadow move toward me as he came back and got in bed behind me, wrapping his arms around me again and pulling my back to his front.

"Sweetest thing I've ever had, Six," he breathed into my neck, giving me a squeeze with his arms then he was out.

I lay there too shocked to wake him and tell him it was me, his steady breathing letting me know that he hadn't a fucking care in the world while the lump in my throat was choking me as I lay there trying to figure out what to do. Wake him? Leave? Punch his fucking lights out?

I couldn't believe he was still pretending that he didn't know it was me and I didn't understand why. We'd just made love (twice) but then he'd acted as if I were someone else.

Oh, God.

I lay there until I was sure I wouldn't start sobbing (or punch his lights out) then moved slowly out of his arms, still completely stunned at his denial. When I sat up, I felt my brow wrinkle as my lips trembled at the sob I was holding back, and I had to bite my lips to hold it in. I got out of bed bending to feel around on the floor for my panties. Upon finding them, I pulled them on then located my robe, covering myself quickly, just wanting to get the hell out of there.

I found my shoes, slipped them on then fled from the room, dodging drunken coeds along the way, and made it across the hallway to the empty (thank God) bathroom I saw. Once inside, I stared at myself in the mirror.

"Idiot," I whispered as a single tear wended its way over my mask and down my cheek.

God, I'd just slept with Gable, the guy I'd fallen for since, oh, who was I fooling, since possibly the moment I'd laid eyes on him, and then he'd gone and acted as if he hadn't known it was me. And now I hated him.

Leaving the bathroom, I immediately saw Bodhi standing tall in the same spot where I'd met Gable, as if he'd been waiting for me, and I went to him, slamming myself into him and wrapping my arms around his waist because I knew the damned tears were coming.

"Hey," he said after a moment, pulling my chin up to look at him.

"We need to go," I answered on a sob.

He nodded then wrapped his arm around me, pulling me to the door and out into the brisk night. We didn't speak until we were in Amy's SUV.

"Amy's staying with Chad," he explained and I felt bad for not even thinking about where she was. He held my door for me then went around to the driver's side and once in, started the SUV. Then he turned to me. "What happened?"

"I don't wanna talk about it right now. Please, Bodhi, just take me home," I answered, still trying to hold back the tears.

He nodded and didn't say another word, just held my hand the entire way to my apartment, squeezing it reassuringly a couple times.

He walked me inside then asked again if I wanted to talk which I definitely did not at that moment, not wanting to relive everything so soon. He told me he had to get to work but to call if I needed anything then kissed my forehead and he was gone.

And I was left to deal with the aftermath of what had happened.

And I was completely devastated.

Week Eleven

I'm not going to say I wasn't a mess after everything that happened because I was. But I was actually proud of how I'd handled things so far. Well, kind of.

I mean, I'd only thrown and broken exactly one glass and one plate and I may also have broken the record in how many cuss words could be said in one sentence, knowing I'd have gotten extra points for throwing in an animal or two with them when Amy and Bodhi had held an intervention two days after the party, which had been Saturday.

I'd moped around the apartment Friday not speaking to either of them, locking myself in my room and sleeping (isn't that what depressed people are supposed to do?), only coming out to use the restroom or get something to drink and when I was safely tucked away again and either of them knocked I told them to go away. This went on until around one in the afternoon on Saturday when Amy finally told me that if I didn't come out and talk, I left her with no other options but to A) call the fire department to axe my door down, B) call the landlord and get the key to unlock my door, C) call Chad to bring his friends and have them bust my door down or D) all of the above.

I wisely came out before any outsiders became involved.

And now Bodhi was busy cleaning up the plate I'd thrown which made me feel horrible so I was helping him. The glass had been earlier and Amy had taken care of it, but I'd been in a huge snit, so it hadn't occurred to me to help.

"I'm sorry," I said as I squatted on the kitchen floor picking up all the pieces. And that was what I was doing, wasn't it? Picking up the pieces of my ridiculous love life.

After we finished cleaning up, we sat at the table and I explained to them what had happened. When I finished, they both stared at me in silence.

"What?" I asked apprehensively.

"Wow," Amy said with a sigh.

"Yeah," Bodhi echoed her breathily.

I narrowed my eyes waiting for them to explain.

"That man's all kinds of sexy, Scout." This was Bodhi commenting.

I sat back in my chair and crossed my arms. "That's not the point, Bode! God! Did you even hear what he did afterward?"

Amy smacked him hard on the arm.

"Hey! What was that for?" he snapped.

"We're supposed to be helping her not swooning over Mr. Hottie and his big dick." She looked at me. "His dick is above average, right? I mean, it'd spoil the whole illusion if he's not packing."

"I'm going back to my room," I huffed and started to stand.

"No! We're sorry!" Amy responded, grabbing my arm and pulling me back down to sit.

I sat then sighed as I stared at the table.

"So what're you gonna do?" Bodhi questioned.

"I don't know," I mumbled, looking up at them.

Amy frowned. "Has he texted?"

I shook my head. "He said we're over, remember?"

"Oh, yeah." Then she asked softly, "Has he emailed?"

I nodded slowly, biting my lips.

"And?" Bodhi said.

I felt my throat get tight. God.

"Honey, what'd he say?" Amy asked quietly, taking my hand in hers and squeezing it.

"He wanted to know why I left without telling him. Then he said he thought he was in love with me." I knew my eyes were shiny with unshed tears when I looked at them.

"That's a good thing, right?" Bodhi offered.

I burst out with a sob, "N—no! He wrote that to *her* not me! He's in love with his pen pal not me," I cried.

Amy handed me a napkin. "But I thought you said he called you Priss?"

I closed my eyes and nodded as the tears slid down my cheeks. "He did, but then he acted like he didn't know it was me." I crossed my arms on the table in front of me and lay my head on them still crying. "I don't know what to do."

They were so quiet I finally looked up to see them having a silent conversation with each other.

"What?" I asked.

Amy cleared her throat. "Yesterday evening when I was leaving for work, Gable showed up here."

"Wh-what?" I stammered, my eyes big with shock. "What'd he want?"

"He said he needed to talk to you, but I, uh, kinda griped him out because I thought he did something to you," Amy replied with a grimace. I just stared at her. "He told me to tell you he came by then he left."

I thought for a second wondering why he'd come by then it hit me and I suddenly felt like I needed to throw up. "Oh, my God," I whispered as my voice hitched. "He was probably coming to tell me he was in love with someone else and that's why he ended it with me. Like, to properly break up with me!" I jumped up from the table so quickly my chair fell over and ran to the bathroom, kneeling down in front of the toilet and gagging.

Bodhi ran in behind me and took my hair in his hands. Amy came in behind him and sat on the tub proceeding to rub my back while I choked out bile. I hadn't eaten in almost two days, so that was a bonus that I wasn't spewing a seven-course meal out in front of my friends. When my stomach finally stopped churning, I sat back, leaning against Amy's legs.

"I'm gonna beat the shit outta him," Bodhi muttered. "He might have more muscle than I do, but I know people and they can fuck him up."

"No!" I cried, mortified, looking up at him. "No. If he doesn't feel anything for me, th—that's not gonna change his mind."

"He's an idiot then," Bodhi retorted.

I took a deep breath and let it out then looked behind me at Amy then back at Bodhi. "What am I gonna do?"

Amy put her hands under my armpits and stood pulling me up with her. She turned me to look at her. "You're gonna hold your head high. Gable Powers is not the be-all, end-all, my gorgeous roomie. The first time you see him, it'll sting a little, but every day after, it'll just get easier and easier." She smiled at me and tucked a piece of hair behind my ear. "And if that doesn't work, Bodhi'll find those friends of his and they'll make Mr. Powers sorry he ever fucked with you, okay?"

Well, that wasn't very soothing, but I gave her a small smile and nodded.

"That's my girl," Bodhi said, taking me in his arms for a big hug.

God, they were the best friends ever.

~*~*~*~

From: 9543254 <student.9543254@hallervan.edu>

Subject: Cinderella

Date: November 2, 10:02 p.m.

To: 9565876 < student.9565876@hallervan.edu>

Six... you ran... why?

Please talk to me...

xx

~*~*~*~

I skipped classes Monday not wanting to run into Gable. I called into work that night not wanting to run into Gable.

Tuesday morning, I skipped classes again not wanting to run into Gable and Tuesday night I called into work again not wanting to run into Gable.

And this went on all week.

"I'm a coward," I said to no one in particular as Bodhi and I sat on the couch in my apartment watching a movie Friday night.

"I agree," he answered.

I sat staring at the TV for a minute before that sank in and I turned my head toward him. "What?"

He shrugged his shoulder and I narrowed my eyes at him. When he didn't say anything, I kept staring knowing he'd finally cave which he did.

"Look, Scout, I understand that you're upset and all. I mean, I would be too. I get it. But you really are being a coward."

I kept staring at him. I knew I was but all I wanted was for him to support me not agree with me.

He sighed and adjusted his glasses then grabbed one of my sock-covered feet and started rubbing it. He always did something nice like that if he was going to give me bad news, like the time he gave me a back rub in the student center then told me he'd come over earlier and eaten the rest of the leftover enchiladas I'd made the night before when I'd been craving them all day long and couldn't wait to get home to have one for dinner.

"I just think it's time for you to move on." He went back to watching whatever movie it was we had on.

I let him keep massaging my foot because it felt good but asked, "And what does that mean? I think I'm allowed at least a week to be upset over sleeping with the guy I was madly in love with who ended up not wanting me but my alter ego, Bodhi." This came out a little snippily but I was rather ticked off just then. But I knew he was right. I was being a brat and needed to suck it up and stop being a baby.

He sighed again. "I know. But here's the deal. Scout, you're freakin' beautiful. You could get any guy you wanted. I just don't want you to get hung up on some idiot who doesn't appreciate you, that's all."

"He's not an idiot," I muttered. Man, I seriously did have it so bad for Gable, so much so that I was sticking up for him even after what had happened.

"If he dumped you, he is."

~*~*~*~

Text Message—Sat, Nov 9, 11:34 a.m.

Gable: You around?

Text Message—Sat, Nov 9, 11:37 a.m.

Gable: I really need to talk to you

Text Message—Sat, Nov 9, 11:44 a.m.

Gable: Scout, please

11:53 a.m.

Gable Calling

Shit. I hit decline and waited to see if he left a voicemail. He didn't. He called back. I declined again and again he called back. This went on for another three times before he finally stopped.

Text Message—Sat, Nov 9, 12:04 p.m.

Gable: I miss you. I'm sorry...

Monday morning I decided to grow up and go to class. Hell, I'd dodged Gable on campus before, I could do it again. Besides, I hated missing even though I'd called and gotten my assignments which I'd hand in when I got to my classes that morning. I'd even emailed five movie reviews to the newspaper last Friday, so that was taken care of.

I made sure to be late to psych as I'd done before, so I could get in, hear the lecture, take notes then be the first to leave which I hoped worked like a charm once again. During class, I avoided looking around the room for fear of seeing Gable, and once Dr. Horner was finished, I booked it the hell out of there without running into him. Thank God.

I was scheduled to work that night, but I'd called Natalie on Saturday and traded for her early shift the entire week, having to fill her in a little on what had happened so she'd give me Gable's schedule and I could summarily avoid him at work too. And that worked in my favor too. Wow. Things were looking up.

Now if only I could avoid him for the rest of my life, everything would be fabulous.

~*~*~*~

Saturday, Bodhi called and asked Amy and me to go out with him that night to a popular club in town because his study group from his History of Anthropological Thought class was going and he thought it'd "Do me good" to get out. I seriously had the best friends in the world.

So I thought, what the hell. I didn't have to work and it wasn't like I was busy having a social life or anything, so Amy and I got "dolled up" (her words), I wore my skinny jeans tucked into my brown riding boots and a sparkly royal blue tank top under a cream chiffon button down shirt. I did my hair and makeup the same way I'd done it for the dreaded

Halloween party, but I'd liked how it'd looked then so, again, what the hell. Amy dressed similarly, looking great as usual, and she was excited because she'd called Chad and he was going to meet her at the club later.

When we were ready, we had a couple tequila shots from the bottle Bodhi had brought over then we all chipped in for a cab. When we got to the club, I showed the fake ID Amy had gotten me a month before, although I knew my dad would pitch a fit if he found out. Oh, well, I didn't have a problem with it because, college, as Amy said and that was good enough for me.

The place was packed with tons of coeds but we managed to find the table Bodhi's group was occupying and he introduced us to everyone, practically having to scream over the loud music, but that was fine. I needed some loudness to drown out the thoughts of Gable that I knew would inevitably sneak up on me throughout the evening. And some of the guys in the group were really cute, and a couple had even asked me to dance, so I was having a great time.

Until I wasn't.

We'd been there a couple hours when a guy named Dawson asked me to dance. We walked to the crowded dance floor and I smiled as we passed Amy who grinned back as she danced with Chad who'd appeared an hour before. Amy was an amazing dancer, her gymnastics having aided with it I'm sure, but when Dawson started dancing, I saw that he was crazy good as he proceeded to show up everyone on the floor. I found myself mostly watching him and grinning because he was fantastic. I mean, people around us were even watching him and some even clapped when the song was over. Wow. Then a slow song came on and I noticed Dawson looking at me with a pouty face which made me laugh. He held his arms out to me, so I stepped into them, raising my left arm up to rest on his right shoulder as he wrapped his right arm around my waist then took my right hand in his left.

"You're really good," I said as we swayed to the song.

"Thanks." He grinned, flashing his perfectly straight, white teeth. "Mom made me take lessons which I hated because I played football and got made fun of on a daily basis. I finally put my foot down when I was fifteen but the damage was already done." He chuckled making me giggle.

"Well, it definitely paid off," I replied smiling up at him.

"If it gets me a dance with a beautiful girl like you, yeah, it has," he said with a wink.

I blushed and ducked my head, and looking off to the side saw Gable staring right at me from a short distance away.

Oh. My. Shit.

My head came up quickly and I saw that he was dancing with a beautiful brunette which made me wheeze in a damned breath.

"I've got to go," I choked out to Dawson then turned and ran off the floor, pushing my way through couple after couple. I didn't even go to the table where Bodhi was to let him know I was leaving, just ran through the club to the front doors and out where I knew they had cabs waiting. I jumped in one and breathlessly gave the guy my address and we took off.

Dramatic? Yes. Necessary? I thought so.

I was working on calming myself down when my phone started buzzing in my back pocket. I twisted my hip and pulled it out to see that Gable was calling. No. No no no no! I hit decline then pulled up a text to Amy and Bodhi to let them know I'd gone and not to worry. After I'd hit Send, my phone buzzed again that Gable had left a voicemail.

God.

I let it go and stared out the window as I was driven through the city to my apartment thinking it was funny how the lights look so much prettier through teary eyes.

When I got to the apartment, I'd already made up my mind and headed directly to my bedroom where I pulled a suitcase out of my closet and began to pack.

Week Thirteen

I'd ended up staying at Bodhi's apartment that night. Since I'd been drinking, I didn't want to be out on the road for too long and his place was only five minutes away, so I'd texted him to make sure it was okay. I hadn't wanted to hang around my place for too long in case Gable showed up because I knew if he did, I probably would've ended up letting him in if not just to scream at him. So I'd packed quickly and had left in under fifteen minutes.

Bodhi had told me his roommate, Grant, would be there, but he'd been asleep when I'd gotten in and he was a nice guy, so I knew he wouldn't have minded anyway. I'd gone right to Bodhi's room and passed out on his bed.

The next morning, I'd awakened when something was tickling my nose, and after swatting at it several times, I finally opened my eyes to see Bodhi lying next to me grinning and holding the pen he'd been using to touch my nose with trying to get me to wake up.

"You jerk," I'd said with a laugh, smacking him on the arm hearing him chuckle as I got out of bed to use his bathroom taking my bag with me so I could brush my teeth. I'd lain back down next to him when I got back to his room.

"Before you texted that you were leaving last night, I knew something was going on because I saw Gable running off the dance floor toward the front," he informed me.

I closed my eyes. "He was dancing with some beautiful woman and I freaked. Am I ridiculous or what?"

"Or what," he said and when I opened my eyes, I saw him smiling sadly at me.

"I pegged him from the start, Bode. He's a player through and through but stupid me had to get all caught up in him." I ran a hand over my face, pulling my hair back into a makeshift ponytail with the band I'd put around my wrist.

"Love makes us do funny things," he said wistfully making me frown at him. "When I saw him going to the front, I followed him."

"You did?"

"Yeah. Some guy who looked just like him, so I'm assuming it was one of the other famous Powers brothers, had come up and Gable started yelling at him, his arms flying all around looking like a crazy man. After he was finished yelling, his brother said something back to him, and Gable just looked so despondent, hanging his head like he'd just lost his best friend. I couldn't help but feel sorry for him."

I sucked in a breath. "You know he lost his best friend years ago. I hate that he was feeling like that."

"You amaze me, Scout," Bodhi said, his eyes warm as he looked at me.

I looked at him like he was a lunatic.

"You're such a good person. And you really do love him."

"That doesn't make me a good person. It makes me a fool," I whispered.

Bodhi shook his head slowly. "I saw Gable leave not long after. Alone."

"Good for him," I muttered not knowing what else to say.

We were over. He'd told me that himself. Then he'd made love to his pen pal, emailing her that he was in love with her. And no matter how much I wanted to believe that he knew it was me, I had to let it go.

Bodhi and I had lain in bed and talked for another thirty minutes about how his night had gone at the club. He'd said he'd met a cute guy and gotten his number, so that was good. They'd made a date for the next weekend and that made me happy for him. He also told me that Dawson had asked for my number but he hadn't given it to him, thank God, because just what I needed was to pull someone else into the freaking madness that was Scout Patterson's idiotic world. We'd ended our conversation with me telling him that I was going home to Stone Springs.

When he'd asked if I was coming back, I didn't have an answer.

After that, we got up and made pancakes eating mostly in silence. When we finished, I cleaned the kitchen while he dressed, and when he came back in, he handed me my bag, frowning at me. I promised him I'd be in contact, gave him a huge hug and left.

And now here I was, back home.

"Scout?" I heard my dad call from the living room.

"Yeah?" I yelled back but got no response, so I got up and went to see what he needed.

"You know I don't carry on conversations from another room."

Yep. I knew that. So great to be home!

"Yeah," I answered.

My dad looked at me, assessing my mood, I guessed, then he spoke. "You up for having dinner at The Ranch tonight?"

The Ranch was a restaurant that my Aunt Hadley owned in town. She wasn't really my aunt but had been my mom's best friend, so that's what my brothers and I called her.

"Uh, yeah. I haven't had awesome food in forever," I replied.

"Then it's a date," Dad said, smiling at me before going back to reading the newspaper he held open in his hands.

I went back upstairs to my room and plopped down on my bed, picking up my phone off my nightstand and texting Amy back since we'd been interrupted when Dad had called.

Text Message—Tues, Nov 19, 2:25 p.m.

Me: Back. Dad and I are gonna eat out tonight. Woohoo. You've got to visit here so I can show you around... it'll take all of five minutes lol

Text Message—Tues, Nov 19, 2:25 p.m.

Amy: ha I'd love to see Stone Springs, Idaho sometime. I'll add it to my Places I'd Never Visit Unless I Was Bored to Friggin' Tears list ;)

Text Message—Tues, Nov 19, 2:26 p.m.

Me: ha Exactly. So anything new going on?

Text Message—Tues, Nov 19, 2:26 p.m.

Amy: Got a new asst mgr at work. She's pretty cool. Didn't make me clean the ice cream machine last night, so that's a plus

Text Message—Tues, Nov 19, 2:26 p.m.

Me: Awesome. Seniority pays off, huh?

Text Message—Tues, Nov 19, 2:27 p.m.

Amy: Yeah, until I work with someone who has seniority over me and she makes me do it ugh

Text Message—Tues, Nov 19, 2:27 p.m.

Me: ha yeah. So I called the university and told them I had an emergency at home and they're allowing me to makeup everything. I'll probably come back the week after Thanksgiving jsyk

Text Message—Tues, Nov 19, 2:28 p.m.

Amy: Good. You need to come back. I miss you. Bodhi misses you : (

Text Message—Tues, Nov 19, 2:28 p.m.

Me: I miss you guys too. Oddly, I miss my classes, even Dr. Rippy's tantalizing lectures in poli-sci about how exciting the Cold War was...

Text Message—Tues, Nov 19, 2:29 p.m.

Amy: I'm sure he holds you spellbound

Text Message—Tues, Nov 19, 2:29 p.m.

Me: Most definitely

Text Message—Tues, Nov 19, 2:30 p.m.

Amy: Okay, let's address the elephant in the room

Text Message—Tues, Nov 19, 2:30 p.m.

Me: Hello, elephant

Text Message—Tues, Nov 19, 2:31 p.m.

Amy: You know what I mean... grrrr

Text Message—Tues, Nov 19, 2:31 p.m.

Me: haha

Text Message—Tues, Nov 19, 2:31 p.m.

Amy: So?

Text Message—Tues, Nov 19, 2:32 p.m.

Me: There's nothing to address... it's over... I mean, he's the one who called it off

Text Message—Tues, Nov 19, 2:33 p.m.

Amy: Scout. He's come by three times. He stalked me all the way across campus the other day just to ask how you were. If he had my # I'm sure he'd cell stalk me too

Text Message—Tues, Nov 19, 2:33 p.m.

Me: I don't know what to tell you

Text Message—Tues, Nov 19, 2:34 p.m.

Amy: Just talk to him jeez

Text Message—Tues, Nov 19, 2:34 p.m.

Me: For what? To hear him, once again, tell me how we're over? Or that he's in love with someone else? I don't need to be reminded.

Text Message—Tues, Nov 19, 2:35 p.m.

Amy: You are one stubborn ass woman #$%^*@

Text Message—Tues, Nov 19, 2:35 p.m.

Me: Are you symbolically cussing me out?

Text Message—Tues, Nov 19, 2:36 p.m.

Amy: I can do the real deal if you want. All I'm saying is give him a chance. I know he's been calling/texting/emailing you, hasn't he?

Text Message—Tues, Nov 19, 2:36 p.m.

Me: Yep

Text Message—Tues, Nov 19, 2:36 p.m.

Amy: And what's he said?

Text Message—Tues, Nov 19, 2:36 p.m.

Me: I don't know. I delete them all

Text Message—Tues, Nov 19, 2:37 p.m.

Amy: Stubborn. Ass. Woman. Jesus

Text Message—Tues, Nov 19, 2:37 p.m.

Me: Bleeding. Heart. Woman. Who. Thinks. Because. She's. In. Love. Everyone. Needs. To. Be.

Text Message—Tues, Nov 19, 2:38 p.m.

Amy: I know. Isn't it great? :P

Text Message—Tues, Nov 19, 2:38 p.m.

Me: It is. I'm really happy for you guys

Text Message—Tues, Nov 19, 2:39 p.m.

Amy: Thanks. I really do love him. He's definitely my next ex-boyfriend

Text Message—Tues, Nov 19, 2:39 p.m.

Me: lol you're so bad. Who knows, things work out, he could be your first ex-husband ;)

Text Message—Tues, Nov 19, 2:39 p.m.

Amy: Gah! That'd be so cool!

Text Message—Tues, Nov 19, 2:40 p.m.

Me: It would lol You crack me up :D K, I'd better go get ready. Dad thinks dinner's at 4. Of course he gets up at 4 am so yeah. Love you. Give Bodhi a big smooch from me!

Text Message—Tues, Nov 19, 2:40 p.m.

Amy: Farmers... ick... Okay. Love you too. I'm not kissing someone who still thinks Pluto is a planet... not even for you...

Text Message—Tues, Nov 19, 2:41 p.m.

Me: Damn. Talk later xo

Text Message—Tues, Nov 19, 2:41 p.m.

Amy: xo

I set my phone down and got up to get ready having not been kidding about Dad eating dinner that early. Before I got to my door, I heard my phone buzz again and went back to pick it up.

Text Message—Tues, Nov 19, 2:42 p.m.

Amy: p.s. give Gable a chance... xo

Uh, yeah. Not happening in this lifetime.

Week Fourteen

The next week passed slowly but I made the most of it, catching up on homework and emailing assignments to my professors.

One afternoon when I'd been extremely bored, all caught up on classwork, Amy was working and Bodhi wasn't answering his texts and Dad had nothing for me to do, I'd finally listened to the voicemail Gable had sent. It'd taken me ten minutes of staring at the unheard message on my phone then another ten trying to think of something else to do, anything, before finally playing it.

Scout, it's me.

And I clicked it off.

God.

God!

I couldn't do it, so I set my phone on the nightstand and opened the drawer, pulling out the tattered vampire romance book I'd read in high school of which I'd earmarked the pages that had all the hot sex scenes on them and that book was earmarked to death. That kept me occupied (and more than a little horny) for the next couple hours until it was time to make dinner.

~*~*~*~

When I'd gone to dinner at The Ranch with Dad the week before, I'd run into Sarah Rudd who'd been co-captain with me our senior year in basketball. She was now attending Gonzaga and majoring in sports medicine. Before she'd left the restaurant, she'd gotten my number and said she'd get hold of a few of our fellow classmates that she knew were in town for Thanksgiving and we could all meet up.

So the next night I went out to the only bar in town, The Liquor Lounge (where the owner never ID'd anyone), meeting up with several friends from high school who I hadn't seen since graduating.

"Scout!" Sarah called out when I walked in.

I gave her a huge hug then made the rounds doing the same with everyone else.

Jordan Cummings had been the beauty queen of our class and was now modeling for several different clothing chains as well as taking college classes online, Wink (yes, Wink) Roberts who'd taken technical classes our junior and senior years was now working as a diesel mechanic for a large farm equipment company, Brady Calhoun had gotten a football scholarship at Oregon and had flown home for a day before he had to go back for practice and then the big game with Oregon State that weekend, and finally Porter Taylor was home from Princeton where he'd received about a million academic scholarships because the guy was a friggin' genius and had led our academic team to the state championship two years in a row.

We'd had a blast reliving old times, practically drinking our weight in alcohol and laughing ourselves sick at some of the ridiculous things that we'd done or that our fellow classmates had attempted during our last three years together.

When we'd left, we'd all wished Brady good luck in the game Saturday then exchanged phone numbers promising to stay in contact.

The next afternoon I attempted listening to Gable's voicemail again. I mean, gee, it'd only taken me forty-eight hours to make another attempt. Not bad. So I pulled up the voicemail then held my breath as I clicked on it.

Scout, it's me. Please listen. I'm an asshole. We really need to talk. Please call me. Please? I'm sorry about everything.

Hm.

Well, that wasn't so bad. Actually, it wasn't bad at all. Man, I must really have been making big strides in the mending of my mangled heart.

So to review his message: he admitted was an asshole, good to know, he wanted me to call him, not gonna happen, and he was sorry. Well, he could go tell it to the brunette he'd been dancing with at the club for all I cared.

Yeah, I know, I was still being a baby, but hey, I figured I had about one more hour to pout then it was time to start acting like a mature adult and move on.

~*~*~*~

"Holy shit, this stuffing is good," Heath said as he jammed another forkful into his mouth.

"Thanks," I answered. "It's a new recipe I found online. It's mostly like Mom's but there's a couple more things added to it." I smiled at him, happy he and Holden could make it home to have Thanksgiving dinner with Dad and me. Heath had brought his new girlfriend, Jocelyn, and I loved her immediately because the minute they arrived, she'd headed straight to the kitchen to help me prepare everything.

I'd gotten up at six that morning to put the turkey in the oven and smiled when I'd looked out the kitchen window to see great big fat snowflakes falling lazily from a gray sky. I'd stayed up to help Dad around the farm some, feeding and watering the horses then helping him to repair a fence. Good times. Once we'd gotten back inside, the snow had started falling pretty heavily and we'd worried that Heath and Holden wouldn't be able to make it, but they had. Holden had flown from Moscow, Idaho, down to Boise last night and stayed with Heath then all three had piled into Heath's four-wheel-drive pickup truck and driven the four and a half hours here without any incident, so thankfully, the snow had been no problem for them.

After eating, we'd sat at the table for a good hour, talking about what was going on in everyone's lives and I realized how much I'd missed them. We laughed so much my stomach hurt, especially when Holden told us about how he'd gotten his case notes mixed up during a mock trial. He said he'd been going on and on during his opening argument about how his (fake) defendant hadn't committed the crime of poisoning the plaintiff's prize-winning pot-belly pig when the trial had actually been in regard to a case where a rather corpulent man was suing an airline for the size of their seats being too small and he hadn't been able to take the flight because he couldn't sit comfortably. When Holden said that in his argument he'd referred to the pig several times over so it'd sounded as if he'd been talking about the plaintiff, I'd about fallen out of my chair, crying with laughter. Oh, God, it was just what I needed, to be with my family and forget about all the shit I'd been dealing with.

Afterward, everyone helped clean up then they all went to the living room to watch football. Since I wasn't particularly interested in any of the games that Holden was switching channels back and forth to, I told Dad I was going to get the tractor and clear the drive. From his turkey coma I heard him mutter (unnecessarily, I might add) for me to dress warmly and to watch the ditches on either side of the driveway. Good grief. I'd cleared the damned thing for years, but I yelled out an "Okay!" throwing in an eye roll as I put on my parka, beanie, scarf and gloves and headed to the barn. The tractor had a heated cab, so once I got inside and it warmed up I could take my coat off, but in the thirty yards I had to walk to get to the barn, I appreciated the coverage.

When the snow had started coming down earlier, Dad and I had attached the snow blade to the tractor just in case, so once I reached the barn, all I had to do was jump in the cab, start that sucker up then get to clearing. Our driveway was pretty long, around a tenth of a mile, and I smiled at that knowing it would take several sweeps to clear it all, which was fine by me because I needed some mindless work to keep my brain occupied. Cranking the radio almost as loud as it would go, I began the mundane but blissful to me task of clearing the snow.

On my third pass, I was rocking out to some Seether when my phone buzzed in my pocket. Twisting in my seat, I pulled it from the back pocket of my jeans... and almost drove into the ditch at what I read.

Text Message—Thurs, Nov 28, 3:06 p.m.

Gable: You look damn sexy driving that huge thing. So badass, Priss

Holy shit.

He was here. Oh, my God. Gable was at my house. In Idaho. On Thanksgiving. And he was texting me.

Holy shit.

My heart seized as I frowned down at my phone not knowing what to do next. But I was proud of how cool I was being not having jerked my head up to look around to see where he was. Nope, I just continued driving as if I hadn't a care in the world, although I did tinker with the idea of doing just that, continuing to drive until I hit the main road then heading to the highway and seeing how far I could go, ala Forrest Gump except for driving and not running. But since that wasn't really feasible, I kept playing it cool, even though I was one-hundred percent freaking out on the inside.

My phone buzzed again but I ignored it, focusing on the task at hand. God, I didn't have time for any of this. I was doing a good job at getting over him. I didn't need him bothering me. I mean, hell, if he wanted to come clear to Stone Springs, Idaho, on Thanksgiving to text me that was his business. I could just as easily not respond to his text whether he was here or ten thousand miles away.

I turned around at the top of the drive nearest the house planning to make my way back down to the end for one more pass when I saw Gable in the black pickup truck I'd first seen him in and he was right in the middle of the road facing me and right in my way. Again, I toyed with an idea that really wasn't appropriate, but I must admit the thought about driving the tractor toward him and not stopping did bring a small smile to my face. But as it was, I sat there, he sat there and we had a visual standoff for a good minute before he grinned at me. Ugh. He next pointed at his mouth then back at me letting me know he wanted to talk to me.

Nope. Not gonna happen. (You might recall what I'd said earlier about the Pattersons being stubborn and bullheaded. Well, there you go.)

So being a Patterson through and through, I put the tractor in reverse and moved back up the drive toward the house, while Gable, of course, followed. Situating the tractor within ten yards of the house, I stopped it, shifted to first and turned off the engine. Then I jumped down from the cab and took off running for the front door of the house.

"Scout!" Gable yelled as he jumped out of the truck, running after me.

I screamed right before he tackled me to the snow-covered ground and when he turned me to face him, I hissed, "Get off me!"

"Not until we talk," he snapped angrily as he glared down at me.

I glared right back at him wondering why he felt he had any right to be mad when he'd clearly been the one to screw everything up. And it was during my glaring that I saw that, damn it, he wore an olive green beanie and now him in a beanie became my new favorite thing ever. Shit.

When he didn't move off me, I scowled up at him, thanking the good lord that I'd kept my coat, hat, scarf and gloves on or I'd be frozen by now from lying in the friggin' snow.

"We gonna lie here all day or what?" I said snidely, my eyes glowering into his.

"You gonna give me a chance to talk?" he asked, eyebrow raised.

"Sure," I lied.

He narrowed his eyes at me probably trying to figure out if I was lying or not but then the idiot decided to trust me and moved off me, standing and offering a hand to help me up but I was already gone, running toward the house and in, slamming the door and locking it.

"What in the world," Dad asked as he sat up in his recliner.

"That guy's trying to get me!" I yelled at Heath and Holden who were on their feet in an instant, moving to the front door quickly to protect their baby sister from whoever was trying to get her. Holden yanked open the door and upon seeing Gable standing there, I shrieked, "Don't let him in!" I got behind Dad's chair, holding on to either side of the back of it hoping my brothers would tell Gable he needed to leave. Well, that or they'd beat the shit out of him for being such an asshole to me. Either worked. But now they'd both gone outside on the porch, closing the door behind them and I stood there trying to catch my breath, waiting to see what they were going to do.

And let me tell you, the disappointment, the betrayal I felt when I saw them both coming inside and bringing Gable with them, and not in a *We're gonna kick this guy's ass for trying to get you* kind of way, hurt my heart immensely. God. Whether they're related to you or not, I'm telling you, you just can't trust men.

Dad had sat quietly as had Jocelyn waiting along with me to see how things would proceed, and when I let out a huff and started to turn and stomp upstairs to my room, Dad moved lightning quick, both his arms coming up to either side of his head and behind him grabbing my wrists that were on his chair keeping me there.

See? You can*not* trust men!

"Dad!" I protested trying to yank my wrists out of his hands, but he only clamped on tighter.

"What's going on here, Scout?" he asked pulling me around to the side of his chair and looking up at me, still holding onto me.

I scowled *so* not wanting to discuss my feelings with my dad… or my brothers… or Jocelyn, whom I'd just met… or with Gable standing right there!

"Nothing," I mumbled. "He's just been harassing me and needs to leave." I glared at Gable whose lips I saw twitch as if he was trying not to grin. Ass.

Dad looked at Gable. "That true, young man?"

Gable cleared his throat. "Well, you see, sir," he began, always the man's man, the big jerk, "I'm in love with your daughter."

Wait.

What?

WHAT!

"But I messed up and hurt her."

Well, jeez, Gable sure didn't have a hard time with sharing his feelings in front of everyone and all I could do was stare at him incredulously.

"And now she can't seem to find time to hear me out or get it into her stubborn head that I'm here to apologize for everything, apologize for acting as if I didn't know she was who I was writing."

Holy cow. Holy cow! He admitted he knew it was me. He finally admitted it! Oh, my God.

Dad looked up at me. "He telling the truth, Scout? You've not given this young man a chance to say what he has to say?"

I frowned down at my dad then raised my head glancing at both Heath and Holden who were looking at me as if a terrible injustice had been performed on my behalf in my not hearing Gable out.

Shit. The level of crazy in the house hit an all-time peak.

I looked at Gable who smirked at me knowing he'd won over the crowd.

Oh, my God.

Okay. Well, two could play this game.

"First of all, he has tattoos. Full sleeves!" I informed them as I stared at Gable, my tone sounding like he'd committed a serious crime.

I saw movement and looked over to see Heath rolling up his sleeve then gasped when I saw he had inkwork started on his arm. Holy shit.

"Wanna try again?" Dad asked.

I huffed because all the wind had been knocked out of my sails but then I rallied. "He's slept with tons of girls! Mostly skanky girls!" I nodded as if this would put an end to this madness.

"Scout," Holden said making me turn his way. "You forgetting how many girlfriends I had in high school?" He grinned at me when I'm sure my face dropped.

I stood stunned at the epic betrayal my family was committing against me right now. And then I got even angrier.

"Are you guys serious right now? Why are you taking his side?" I screeched. And then to my mortification, I kept going. "He... he... he slept with me then acted as if he didn't know it was me! Then he danced with another woman *right in front of me!*"

The room got very quiet. Then I heard Holden snort which made me turn my glare on him at which he just grinned. God!

"Scout," Dad said, dropping his hands from my wrists, turning in his chair to see me more clearly.

Oh, lord. I was in serious shit now for letting that cat out of the bag.

I looked down at him with a wince waiting to hear how I'd be grounded until I was at least fifty.

Dad closed his eyes and took a deep breath then opened them, looking up at me. "Although I hate the idea of my little girl not saving herself for marriage," he pinned me with his steely gray eyes making me bite my lip nervously. "I think I know you well enough that you're not one of these *skanks* that you mentioned and you'd only give yourself to someone you cared about." Now his eyes landed on Gable and I hoped he was going to lay down the law to him. "But, young man, if I find out you've used my daughter in any way after engaging in amorous congress with her, then you're treading on thin ice right about now."

Amorous congress? What the hell?

"I love her, Mr. Patterson," Gable answered, looking my dad right in the eyes.

"Well, then, it seems as if you'll pass muster," Dad said, getting up out of his chair. "We'll give you two a chance to talk. Boys, how about driving into Idaho Falls with me to pick up a Christmas tree? I'm sure Jocelyn has a fine eye and will keep me from getting a Charlie Brown version like I did last year." He patted my arm with a chuckle then I watched in disbelief as they all went to the front door pulling their coats off the coat rack, donning them and out the door they went leaving Gable and me alone.

Again, what the hell?

I now heard Gable chuckle and my eyes slid to his, and, believe me, I was not happy with how things had just gone down.

"Are you kidding me right now?" I hissed as I glowered at him.

"Seems as if I'll pass muster," he said, his eyes looking at me in amusement.

I huffed again. "Just because my dad thinks that, it doesn't mean I do," I replied keeping the glower going.

"Scout... I'm sorry." He took a step toward me.

"You stay right where you are, Gable Powers," I demanded, pointing my finger at him. "You..." I swallowed the lump that had risen in my throat. "You hurt me," I whispered as tears stung the backs of my eyes.

I saw the remorse on his face when he said, "I know I did, and I'm so sorry."

"Why?" I asked, wanting to know his reasoning behind it all. And not able to keep my emotions in check any longer, I felt my lips trembling as a tear escaped to roll its way down my cheek. I don't think I'd ever been hurt so badly before.

He took a few more wary steps toward me and I just didn't have it in me to stop him. So taking full advantage of my weakness he kept coming toward me until suddenly I was in his arms.

"Baby, I'm so sorry," he said against the side of my head as he held me. "I was an idiot. I was scared."

I pulled away but he kept his hands on my waist not letting me get too far from him. My hands went to my face to wipe away the tears then I rested them on his forearms and looked up at him. "Why were you scared?"

He sighed, looking pained then he shook his head. "I've had only one serious girlfriend, Scout. Her name was Mia and she hurt me bad. She said she loved me but couldn't accept me as I am. It got old really fast, so I broke it off with her."

"Uh, I know this," I said quietly. He frowned down at me. "Don't be mad at him, but I asked Loch." I saw Gable's eyes get hard. "It wasn't his fault!" I explained. "I kinda cornered him. He thought I was your girlfriend and deserved to know, so he told me."

I watched a flood of emotions move over his face then he seemed to come to terms with things as he nodded. "Then you know what happened... know she'd been cheating with my best friend... before they died..."

I looked at him sadly and gave him a slight nod.

"Got the fucking tattoo in honor of him before I knew about them," he said with a humorless laugh. "But it's become a grim reminder not to trust anyone."

I bit my lips as I watched him, a frown on his beautiful face as he tried to work out the demons he had inside. Then he looked at me and his eyes were suddenly soft, warm.

"But you were different. You accepted me. Took all my shit I threw at you trying to keep you away." He brought a hand up and cupped my jaw, smoothing his thumb over my bottom lip staring at it. Then his eyes moved up to mine. "You took all the bad inside me and replaced it with hope. Woke me up... made me feel something again."

"Gable—" I started.

"Loved me for who I was... you gave that all back to me... and that scared me shitless..."

"Gable—"

He dropped his hand back to my waist, his eyes intense on mine. "You gave me stitches, Scout."

Oh, my God.

Oh, my God!

"Gable—" I whispered.

"Thought if I could just be with you, I'd get you outta my system. Should've known better." His eyes held mine. "I'm with you, Scout." I knew he saw the alarm on my face since I'd already heard that one right before he'd broken things off with me and my head dropped. His hands shot out to cup my face, pulling my chin up so I'd look at him. "I'm with you, baby. God, I'm so sorry I hurt you. Can you forgive me?"

I looked up at him seeing that his eyes were so sincere, so how could I not? I loved him and that's what people did when they loved someone, they forgave. So I tiptoed up, my hands moving to rest against his chest, and touched my lips to his. "You're forgiven," I said against his mouth and felt the relief rolling off him.

"I love you, Scout," he said then his mouth took mine hard, his arms wrapping around my waist as he pulled me into him tightly.

He made love to me in my bed, promising that he'd do everything in his power never to hurt me again.

Yes, I'd have to say he passed muster.

Week Seventeen

From: 9543254 <student.9543254@hallervan.edu>

Subject: Fair warning

Date: December 16, 7:12 a.m.

To: 9565876 < student.9565876@hallervan.edu>

Six,

I'm a little wary about the reveal thing we're about to do in psych class today. I mean, I think you're cool and all, but I *do* have an extremely jealous girlfriend and I don't think she'd like the fact that I'm meeting another woman. I mean, she got mad that I was dancing with my brother's girl while he took a piss for chrissakes.

But I will tell you she's crazy about me and all because, as you know, I'm smokin' hot, so I'm warning you now to try to keep your hands off me, although the temptation will be great I'm sure. If you can't resist, she might be inclined to kick your ass if you try to move in on her man. Just fair warning.

xo

From: 9565876 < student.9565876@hallervan.edu>

Subject: Cocky SOB

Date: December 16, 7:14 a.m.

To: 9543254 <student.9543254@hallervan.edu>

Dear Mr. Four,

Thank you for the warning. I'll make sure to keep myself in check as I know that your extreme hotness and my inability to resist it could cause quite the uproar on campus if I were to throw you to the floor right there in the middle of class and have my wicked way with you.

That being said, I might warn you too that since our epistolary relationship has now come to an end, you'll no longer be receiving my amorous congress through the written word. I hope your girlfriend will be able to fill that void in your corporeal world.

Please don't try to contact me after today because I too have a significant other who, although I haven't given him reason to be jealous, might not like it if we kept this tête-à-tête going. Therefore, I regret to inform you that you're old news.

Later.

From: 9543254 <student.9543254@hallervan.edu>

Subject: Cold-hearted wench

Date: December 16, 7:20 a.m.

To: 9565876 < student.9565876@hallervan.edu>

Jesus, Scout...

You're killing me here. I'm now jealous over a fucking number.

I'm coming over to claim what's mine. Be ready.

See you in ten.

From: 9565876 < student.9565876@hallervan.edu>

Subject: Cro-magnon cave dude

Date: December 16, 7:20 a.m.

To: 9543254 <student.9543254@hallervan.edu>

No need to be jealous, baby. There's only you. Always.

And, believe me, I'm ready. Your email woke me up while I was having an awesome dream about you.

Come take what's yours.

From: 9543254 <student.9543254@hallervan.edu>

Subject: Holy fuck

Date: December 16, 7:21 a.m.

To: 9565876 < student.9565876@hallervan.edu>

>Fuck me...

>Leaving now.

>Taking Ryke's car. I left the windows down on the Chevelle. It's all wet inside so I'll have to get in there and take care of it later

---

From: 9565876 < student.9565876@hallervan.edu>

Subject: Boom!

Date: December 16, 7:22 a.m.

To: 9543254 <student.9543254@hallervan.edu>

>That's what she said...

Epilogue

You know that feeling you get when you meet someone and feel as if you've known them for a lifetime? As if you're just connected in some way?

Totally had that when I first saw Scout.

God, she was the most beautiful woman I'd ever seen. And the sassiest. And I loved it.

I don't know what caused me to stop to help with her tire when I'd actually been on a date with someone else, but I thank God each and every day that I did. In all my life, she's the only person outside my family who's truly accepted me for who I am and that means everything to me.

Oh, it took me a while to get to where I am today but I'd go back and do everything the same if it got me to this place with her. Yes, I figured out she was my pen pal when she came to class hungover. But I was just a terrified prick who didn't know how to have her goodness in my life after all the hurt I'd experienced. I should've known she'd figure it out.

But I'm not gonna waste your time here with some sappy interlude about how it all went down and how I screwed up (because that would take hours), but I am gonna tell you I'm the luckiest bastard there is for how everything turned out.

I did thank Dr. Horner in my thesis for making us do this assignment because without it, I'd never have landed the most wonderful, fabulous and amazing woman in the world. Who knew I'd actually get something out of a class?

So to wrap this up (told you it wouldn't be long) I just want to say, don't ever lose your hope. I did and Scout brought it back to me. I owe her everything. But even if you do, there's always a way to get it back.

Okay, I'm gonna end this now before my brothers get a hold of it and give me hell. And believe me, they'd make me suffer. Long and hard.

And you guessed it...

That's what she said.

Watch for Zeke (The Powers That Be, Book 2) coming September 2015!

About the author:

Harper Bentley has taught high school English for 22 years. Although she's managed to maintain her sanity regardless of her career choice, jumping into the world of publishing her own books goes to show that she might be closer to the ledge than was previously thought.

After traveling the nation in her younger years as a military brat, having lived in Alaska, Washington State and California, she now resides in Oklahoma with her teenage daughter, two dogs and one cat, happily writing stories that she hopes her readers will enjoy.

You can contact her at harperbentleywrites@gmail.com, at harperbentleywrites.com, on Facebook or on Twitter @HarperBentley

Discover other titles by Harper Bentley:

CEP series:

Being Chased (CEP #1)

Unbreakable Hearts (CEP #2)

Under the Gun (CEP #3) coming March 2015!

Serenity Point series:

Bigger Than the Sky (Serenity Point Book 1)

Always and Forever (Serenity Point, Book 2) coming June 2015!

True Love series:

Discovering Us (True Love #1)

Finding Us (True Love #2)

Finally Us (True Love Book 3)

http://harperbentleywrites.com/

Made in the USA
Lexington, KY
17 October 2015